Three Summers On

Heartlines

Heartlines

Jill Young

Three Summers On

A Pan Original

First published 1986 by Pan Books Ltd,
Cavaye Place, London SW10 9PG
9 8 7 6 5 4 3 2 1
© Jill Young, 1986
ISBN 0 330 29354 0

Printed and bound in Great Britain by
Hunt Barnard Printing, Aylesbury, Bucks

Chapter 1

'You'll be okay, Nell,' Mark said. He then did an amazing thing. He kissed me. Not on the mouth or anything lush like that but on my cheek. Even so I nearly flipped. Standing right there under the hollow oak we kids used to hide in I nearly croaked from joy.

'I hope you're right,' I said when I could breathe again.

'Of course I am. You're going to do great things. Be someone.'

'Think so?'

'I know so. You've come a long way in the past few months. Keep it up and you should have no trouble with your O levels. This time next year you may even decide to tackle your As. If you want to know, I'm really proud of you.' He grinned and my heart turned a somersault. 'One day I'll be able to boast of having known the famous Nell Carter.'

Tittering inanely, I swung on a low overhanging branch. I mean what do you say when someone you fancy like mad compliments you like that?

Mark slipped the key into the lock of his car. 'Doing anything special this summer?'

For a wild moment I thought he might suggest our meeting or something but that was crazy. He was twenty-seven to my sixteen and the best-looking guy around Hobleigh. More to the point he was the social worker assigned to me after Mum did the bunk, in the hope — so far unfulfilled — of getting me back into school.

'Dunno yet,' I said. 'Dad has this idea of my going to work for friends of Mrs Lawton at their place in Dorset.'

'Really? I know Peggy Lawton and her antique shop well.'

'It's a holiday centre for handicapped kids.'

He stopped fiddling with the door of his new car and looked thoughtful. 'That would be good experience.'

'Yeah, maybe.' Moodily I scuffed the ground with the toe of my trainer.

'What's wrong, then?'

I shrugged. 'Nothing really.' I could hardly tell him that I'd prefer to stick around Hobleigh on the off chance of bumping into him in the shopping precinct or the sports centre.

'You going anywhere particular?' I asked, hoping he would say no.

'Bet your life I am.' His blue eyes sparkled. 'Crete. Swimming, windsurfing, lazing around the tavernas and beaches. That's the life after a hard winter.'

I forced a weak grin. 'Have a great time.'

'Thanks.' He got into the car and lowered the window. 'By the way, I've been meaning to tell you — apropos our many chats on the subject — you won't have to brave school on the first day alone next term. M'lady will be chauffeured from door to door.'

I pulled a face. 'Escorted, you mean. Bound, gagged and handcuffed!'

He gave me a level blue look. 'No one is going to force you to go back to school, Nell, but if you want to sit your Os you'd give yourself a better chance in class than studying at home with a tutor — even one as good as Mr Steadman.'

'I don't see why.' I did, of course, but it was a legit ploy to keep him talking a while longer. Once he drove away I wouldn't see him again for nearly two months.

He gave a mock sigh and ran his hand through his thick fair hair. 'We've been over all this before. Because you'll be able to pace yourself against the others; toss your ideas around and get the feedback. You've been working in isolation for nearly three years and it's now time you pitched in with the rest. You agreed with the psychiatrist about that. You've got to make the effort to go back to school before you get a permanent hang-up about, well, about everything that made you ill three years ago. After all, when you are a business tycoon . . .'

I snorted. 'Ho-ho. Very funny. Go peddle your jokes in the tavernas. The other tourists might appreciate them!'

He laughed. 'You're not the toughie you pretend to be, Nell. In some ways you're a bit of a fraud. Anyway, I've thoroughly enjoyed working with you. You've been a smashing client and I'll keep an ear open for your future successes.'

'If any!'

'Oh I don't think you need worry about that,' he laughed, and raising a hand in a farewell salute he spurred the engine and zoomed away, leaving a cloud of dust hanging in the sultry afternoon air.

Wandering back up the path I asked myself about that kiss. Why today? He'd never kissed me before. It was almost as though he'd been saying goodbye. Well, I reasoned, of course he had. He was off to Crete and I was off to Dorset. Closing my eyes I relived the closeness of him, the spicy smell, the pressure of his lips against my cheek. Bliss. Even so, a vague uneasiness stirred inside me as I entered the house.

Dad was making tea in the kitchen. He always did his share around the place, I'll say that for him. In the three years following Mum's disappearing act he had never shirked the chores or expected me to do everything, although most of the other men around Hobleigh came home and fell dead in front of the telly until their tea was plonked on to the table.

Before Mum went off Dad did the same, so perhaps she just got fed up with making tea for a corpse. I dunno. Anyway, I still thought about her often. It was *not knowing* that was the worst — whether she was alive or dead, I mean. Sometimes I almost wished she was dead because of what she'd done — *abandoning us* like that. I mean Dad's not exactly a monster. He's quiet and not bad looking if you go for small fair men with thin, lined faces. He's much stronger than he looks, too. Wiry. Trouble is he hardly ever says anything. Sometimes I think he must have taken a vow of silence at birth. Mum on the other hand always nattered twenty to the dozen, so you had to shout to make yourself heard. It never bothered Dad. He just ignored her. It really got up her nose to be ignored and I've seen her empty his cornflakes over his head, milk and all. No, I mean it. All he did was wipe the stuff off, grab his jacket and light out through the door, followed by me in double quick time. She wasn't too nice to be near when she was like that.

Dad worked at Pierce's ironmongers in the High Street.

Mr Pierce was always joking that he was worth his weight in iron filings. So ask for a rise, I told him, but he just shook his head and muttered about being lucky to have a steady job at fifty-two. Honestly, remarks like that make me spew up.

Anyway, I took over washing the lettuce because the way he did it you were likely to end up with half Hobleigh Market Garden between your fillings.

'Thought any more about going to that place for handicapped kids?' he asked when we'd sat down to eat.

I shrugged. 'A bit.' Then I took a leaf out of Mark's book. 'Might be good experience.'

He gave me a sharp look – as if he thought I might be taking the mickey – but I paid no attention. Inside my head I was picturing Mark as he drove away in the red Metro, his hand raised in that farewell gesture, the gold signet ring glinting on his finger. Wait a minute. I knew something was bothering me. Surely I hadn't seen that ring before? Yet I must have. People don't suddenly start flashing new rings around unless it's a birthday or something. It wasn't Mark's birthday until December. Another thing – he hadn't said 'See you soon' like he usually did. But he had joked about chauffeuring me to school for the first time, which amounted to the same thing.

'I wonder when Mrs Lawton's friends want me to start work,' I mused aloud.

Dad flipped to the sporting page of the local rag. 'You'd better get round to her shop and find out – if you're serious.'

'Course I'm serious. But if I go will you be okay? Six weeks is a long time.'

He grunted scornfully. 'It'll pass like castor oil through the canary.'

'Dad! Must you?'

Honestly – he can be crude at times.

Chapter 2

Peering through the windows of Mrs Lawton's antique shop I spotted her working in the tiny office at the back of the showroom, so after padlocking my bike I rang the bell. She opened up at once without looking to see who it was. Stupid really. I could have been any kind of a nutter.

'Nell, what a lovely surprise!' She cried as if I was her long-lost cousin or something. 'You've chosen the right time to call. I've just made a fruit cake.'

It was all I could do not to turn tail and flee. Mrs Lawton's fruit cakes are notorious in Hobleigh. They turn up everywhere, even at the local Antique Fair. I don't know who buys them because you can only use them as door-stops. Anyway, I followed her through to the kitchen while she gushed on about how pretty I'd grown. Needless to say I lapped it up. Who wouldn't?

'You've got your mother's gorgeous green eyes and blonde hair, Nell. Lucky you. And your father's long legs. I bet you run like a hare.'

She was right there; running's one thing I do well, but I did wish she hadn't mentioned Mum. I hated it when people did that, pretending nothing was wrong and she was still around like other mums. Mrs Lawton meant it kindly, though. Normally I distrust gushy people because you never know what they are like underneath, but she's the exception. She's okay. Mr L.

had died about six months earlier and she seemed to have got a lot gushier since then. I think she was lonely.

A saggy cake weighed down the kitchen table.

'Let's cut a slice each,' Mrs L. said.

'Thanks Mrs Lawton but I've just finished my tea,' I bleated feebly. I mean I hated to discourage the old thing.

Her face fell. 'Don't tell me you don't want any.'

'No, no . . . (coward) . . . I certainly *want* some. It's just that I'm a bit full.'

'Oh I expect you can manage a piece,' she insisted, cutting me a hunk the size of Westminster Abbey.

She led me through to her sitting room. It was stuffed with old photographs and pretty knick-knacks all lying about on tiny tables and it smelt of flowers and polish. The flowers had dropped their petals everywhere so the furniture looked adrift in a sea of yellow confetti.

'Did you want to see me about something special?' she asked when we were settled with our plates on our knees.

'It's that job in the children's holiday centre. You see, if it's still on I'd like to go.'

'I am glad,' she said, bouncing up and down excitedly – which bothered me a bit since she must tip the scales at fifteen stone and the chair is a genuine Victorian job.

'You'll have a lovely time,' she enthused. 'It will be hard work but I've got a feeling you'll get along well with the children. Several local girls work for Bill and Jane, so you won't have to look far for friends. Do you like goat's milk yoghurt?'

'Goat's milk . . .' I choked on a burnt raisin. 'I don't know.'

'I'm sure you do. They make their own at Finchings.

It's quite near the sea, so you'll be able to go swimming in your free time. Oh Nellie it will be so good for you to get away for a few weeks.'

I hate being called Nellie but you can't help liking Mrs Lawton.

'When do they want me to start?' I asked.

'As soon as possible, I should think. They are very short-staffed. Anyway, I'll find out and let you know. I don't imagine your father can take much time off work, so I'll drive you down myself. Doesn't my garden look splendid?'

She had this amazing habit of leaping from subject to subject. You practically had to be a mind-reader to keep up with her.

'It looks great,' I said. Through the glass doors I could see masses of blowzy roses and spiky blue delphiniums growing each side of a lavender-edged path. Stratford, her ginger cat, was crouching on the path, meanly eyeing a butterfly. I'd have hurled my cake at him had Mrs Lawton not been there.

'What a good thing you are now well enough to go back to school next term,' she said, brushing the cake crumbs off her bosom. 'I expect you'll miss your visits from Mark Field, though. How exciting for him to be getting married and going off to live in Leeds.'

'Leeds? Mark?' Something must have gone wrong with my hearing.

'Yes. Apparently that's where his fiancée lives. She is a teacher and they decided it would be easier for him to get a job in the social services there than for her to find one here. Of course he is very dedicated. Look how much time he has devoted to you since your illness. I'm afraid Hobleigh will miss him, though. We'll hear more of that young man, mark my words. Oh dear, what a terrible pun!' And she went off into gales of laughter.

I shook my head disbelievingly. 'Excuse me, Mrs Lawton, but I think you've got it all wrong. Mark Field is going to Crete soon but he's definitely coming back to Hobleigh. You see, he's going to drive me to school on the first day of term because I'll be very nervous about going in alone. He knows that. We talked about it. He promised. It's all arranged.'

The bright expression on Mrs Lawton's face kind of fell apart, disintegrated like an old building under demolition, and she covered her mouth with her hand as if to stop any more words escaping. A thick gold band gleamed dully on her finger and all of a sudden I had a vision of Mark's shiny new ring as he'd waved goodbye.

'It's all arranged,' I repeated loudly and the next thing I knew, these huge tears were pouring down my face on to my new sailcloth skirt and my plate had fallen and smashed to smithereens on the parquet floor.

'Oh my dear . . .' Mrs Lawton suddenly sank to her knees and tried to gather me into her arms but I fought her off, yelling, 'It's all arranged. Don't you see? It's a mistake. He promised . . . '

But Mrs Lawton — who's really strong when she wants to be — gripped me in a steely embrace moaning 'It's all my fault. It's all my fault.' (If she said it once she said it a million times.) 'I had no idea you didn't know. No idea.' (She said that a million times, too.) 'You'll get over it, my dear. Give it time. Gve it time. Oh Lord, what a clumsy old woman I am!'

Funny thing. Being wrapped in Mrs Lawton's arms and smelling her scent and all that made me cry harder than ever. I suppose it was because she felt warm and soft and safe; which reminded me of Mum except that Mum never kissed or cuddled me. Soppy she called it. Anyway I bawled my head off and she went on calling herself every kind of a fool until, eventually, I dried up and she sat back on her heels, her hair all awry and her eyes swimmy with distress.

'Sorry about the plate,' I hiccupped. 'I'll pay for it out of my first pay cheque.'

She looked unhappier than ever. 'Of course you won't. I'll never forgive myself for blundering on like that. And after all you've been through, too.'

By that I suppose she meant Mum doing the vanishing trick and my breakdown.

'He should've told me,' I said dully. 'Mark should've told me he was going.'

'I expect he had his reasons,' she said gently. 'Perhaps he knew it would upset you and he just got cold feet. It's understandable. Anyway, when you are safely back at school you'll realize that you don't need him any more.'

She didn't understand. I didn't blame her – she was old. Love and all that must have seemed ancient history to her. I *did* need Mark. I needed to talk to him knowing that he would really listen, really care. I just needed to spend a couple of hours a week with him like I had for the past three years. It wasn't much to ask. But now all that was over. Everything that had renewed my life, made it bearable again after Mum left, was finished. I felt dry and empty but at the heart of the emptiness a sneaky seed of anger was sprouting rapidly. Soon it would have nowhere to expand and it would explode. I must get away before it happened.

'I'd better go now,' I said, getting up abruptly.

Mrs Lawton struggled to her feet. 'Are you sure you're all right?'

I forced a tight smile. 'Yeah, I'm fine. Really.'

She looked unconvinced. 'Well, I'll pop over tomorrow and tell you when Jane and Bill want you to start at Finchings.'

I frowned. 'Well, I . . .'

'Now you're not going to change your mind are you?'

'I dunno. N-no. I suppose not.'

'Of course you're not,' she said briskly. 'Mark Field – and a whole team of others let us not forget – has done his best for you and now he is going to marry the girl he loves and go off to help someone else. You must try to be glad for him. Nell? You will, won't you?'

I nodded but I didn't say 'yes'; that would have been too much.

I needed to be alone, so instead of going home I biked along to the cricket field and sat on the pavilion steps. The grass had just been cut and still had that sharp tickly smell. The sun was going down behind the apartment blocks at the back of the field, sinking slowly between the roof-tops as if God, or someone, was too tired to hold it up any longer.

Mark should have told me. He should. Instead he deliberately allowed me to think he would be around in the autumn. I hate people who let you think one thing when all the time they know something else. It's cheating. Well, I could cheat too. I would go gack on my word and not return to school. After all, I was sixteen and could leave any time I wished. The law said so. If Mark was so keen for me to take my Os and do great things he should have stayed to support me. Now he would never be able to boast about knowing the famous Nell Carter. Instead he'd have to take the blame for another unemployment statistic, and if he heard about my wasted life so much the better.

The sun plopped out of sight behind the block of flats, leaving me on the edge of a dark green void.

'Oh Mark,' I whispered, 'please don't forget me.'

But an owl hooted in the shadows and I felt mocked and lonely in a hostile world.

Chapter 3

When I was younger we sometimes went to Blackpool for a week in the summer. Mum loved it. She had a big thing about amusement parks. Plunging roller-coasters and other death-defying rides really turned her on and I think she despised me for hating them and trotting off to the kid's boating pool. Anyway those were the only occasions I'd ever been away from home, so it felt strange to be leaving Hobleigh knowing I wouldn't see it again for six weeks.

When we'd been driving for about an hour Mrs Lawton said, 'You're quiet today Nell. Are you nervous?'

'No,' I lied. 'It's just too hot to talk.'

The glaring surface of the road ahead seemed to shift and shimmer, and the air rushing through the window felt like a desert wind.

'Won't it be lovely to reach the sea?' she sighed as we

stopped at the lights in the bustling centre of a crowded town.

'Yes,' I agreed absently. I was thinking how different – how happy I suppose – everyone looked ambling around in the sun, pushing prams packed with fat babies or sitting on benches licking ice-creams. Suddenly I was desperate for a raspberry ripple but I didn't like to ask Mrs Lawton to stop, so to take my mind off it I mentioned something that had been bothering me.

'By the way, have you told Bill and Jane about me?'

'What about you?'

'Well, about Mum going off and me dropping out of school and all that.'

She looked shocked. 'Certainly not. It's none of their business. Anyway, you are going back next term so all that's water under the bridge.'

I didn't reply. I was still determined not to return, but so far I hadn't told anyone. Dad was so set on my getting some Os and going to college that he'd be bound to blow a fuse. It would be better to get a job first and have everything settled before breaking the news.

We could smell the sea long before we saw it, and sticking my head out of the window I gulped in the ozoney air. Then we rounded a corner and there it was, a sheet of sparkling, silvery water dotted with white foam-flecks, stretching away beyond the dry fields and dusty, wind-bent trees. Soon it was lost in the curve of the road but the brief glimpse had been exciting enough to drive away all desire for a raspberry ripple.

'I envy you,' Mrs Lawton said. 'I wish I were spending this glorious summer at Finchings.'

'Wiping kid's noses and making goat yoghurt?' I asked innocently.

She laughed. 'No. Lying in the shade, sipping lemonade served by you.'

The private drive to Finchings was about a mile long and as the old car bumped merrily in and out of the deep ruts I caught the gleam of water between some trees away on the left.

'Is that a lake?' I asked.

Mrs L. smiled mysteriously. 'I'm not telling you a thing. That way you'll have the pleasure of discovering it all yourself.'

The house was built of rose-coloured bricks and had lots of huge sash windows, long enough for a person to walk in and out of instead of using the door. Deep yellow roses scrambled all over the walls and my first thought was: imagine being able to call a place like this home!

We circled the house and drove into a cobbled yard at the rear. Before the car had even stopped two people appeared and walked towards us. The woman was thin and dark and casually dressed in jeans and a long blue-and-white striped apron. The man, distinctly plump, had floppy hair (going bald) and pale blue eyes. He also wore jeans, although, to be frank, he didn't look too good in them. Flinging open the car door he threw his arms around Mrs Lawton.

'Peggy darling – how gorgeous! Doesn't she look radiant, Jane?'

'Radiant,' Jane agreed, dropping a light kiss on Mrs L.'s flushed cheek.

'Oh you flatterers,' she said, pleased as a cat with a tin of sardines.

'And you must be Nell,' Jane said, turning to me.

I nodded and grinned but couldn't think of what to say, so I got out of the car and began to drag out my case. I liked Bill's round cheerful face but wasn't so sure about the pallid Jane, who stood there looking me up and down as if I were a prize heifer or something.

'She doesn't look very strong,' she said doubtfully.

'She just needs fattening up, that's all,' Bill said, taking my case.

'Poor Nell,' laughed Mrs Lawton. 'She'll think you're planning to send her to market or something.'

Jane gave me a friendly grin and instinct suddenly told me that she would be easier to handle than Bill.

My room was in the converted stables a short distance from the house and Bill carried my case across while Jane took Mrs Lawton into the house.

Bill pushed open a door at the head of the narrow stairs. 'This is yours,' he said putting down my case. 'I hope you won't be lonely.'

It was a small, sparsely furnished room with a cork-tiled floor, a bed with flowered cover, a bow-fronted chest of drawers, a writing table and a chair with a cane seat.

'Hanging space behind this,' Bill said, pulling aside a flower-sprigged curtain. 'Sorry it isn't more luxurious but we're not exactly running a hotel.'

'It's great,' I said. I mean it really was.

He smiled, gratified by my appreciation. 'Then make yourself at home. When you've unpacked come over to the house for lunch and meet the children. They know you are coming and they are bursting with curiosity. Take this afternoon to settle in and look around the place but the tempo speeds up at supper time so we'd be glad of your help then.'

When he'd gone I sat on the bed and hugged myself with pleasure. My very own room in this amazing old stable block. What fabulous luck! For the first time in my life I was really on my own and was I going to make the best of it!

Quickly I put away my stuff and changed into a white cotton skirt and a turquoise sun top, silently blessing Dad for being as generous as he could with money for clothes before I came away. Standing in front of the mirror I brushed my short blonde hair until it stood in a soft cloud around my head, then I debated whether or not to touch up my eyes but decided against it. I'm lucky enough to have large green eyes with dark gold lashes which don't need make-up. I'll never need blusher either because I have a rosy skin. Too rosy at times.

After changing I stood by the low window looking into the stable-yard. Years ago, when the boxes were filled with horses, grooms and stable lads would have been scurrying around shouting, laughing, swearing. You would have heard the stamp of hooves on tiles, and smelt the piles of steaming straw. Now it was so quiet that you could hear the doves gently cooing in their cote on the roof, and instead of snorting, whinnying horses the stables were filled with garden tools and light farm machinery. Spotting the back of a tractor I wondered if I'd be allowed to learn to drive it.

As I gazed out of the window a boy of about eighteen or nineteen wearing navy dungarees crossed the yard. He had straight black hair which gleamed in the sunlight and the skin of his face and hands looked brown, as if he spent a lot of time outside. Almost as though he sensed my presence he glanced up at the window and we stared at each other. He was tall and had black shiny eyes under a swinging fringe, and a wide mouth which tucked in at the corners giving his face a secretive air. I knew he hadn't expected to see me because his expression was one of stunned amazement. I laughed. Well, I couldn't help it, he looked so funny. Then he scowled, picked up an empty bucket and trudged away under the arched entrance.

Chapter 4

The dining room was one of the rooms with long windows at the front of the house. Like the rest of the house, however, it was not grandly furnished. The floor had bare boards and we sat at round tables with formica tops. The children – about a dozen of them – were divided three or four to a table with a staff member to provide help for those who needed it – and some of the more handicapped did.

I was put with Jane and two girls of about ten and eleven who were born with Down's Syndrome. Sitting with us was a beautiful little boy who was blind and deaf and couldn't hold up his head properly. Of course he had to be helped with his food. At first I couldn't understand what the girls said but Jane translated for me and after a while I more or less got the hang of their speech. Diane kept reaching across the table for my hand and I was all for letting her hold it but Jane said firmly that it was lunchtime and hand-holding could come later. Rachel was the shy one and kept looking at me from under long brown lashes and giggling. She was so funny that she soon had me giggling too, then Diane started, then Jane. After a bit Ricky, who must have felt our vibes, started yelling with laughter and banging his spoon on his plate. We were a very noisy table.

Although I could have cried at the state of some of the kids the feeling didn't last long because they were all so happy. Everyone was happy. It didn't matter who knocked over their mug of water or sloshed food on to the floor, no one minded, and by the end of the meal I was quite at home and knew I was going to enjoy my spell at Finchings.

After lunch Mrs Lawton said she'd better be going, so I walked to the car with her. The heat inside was oven-like and we opened the door to cool it down.

'Now, Nell, do you think you'll be happy here?' she asked anxiously.

'I'm sure I will. The kids are so lovely.'

'And do you think you'll get along all right with Bill and Jane? You'll have to be patient if anyone snaps at you. From time to time everyone gets a bit tired.'

'Don't worry. I can see how it is.'

'That's all right then. Just do your best.'

'I will; and Mrs Lawton . . . thanks for everything.'

She kissed me and got into the car while I shut the doors.

'Goodbye, Nell.'

Waving like crazy, I ran down the drive after the battered Morris until it disappeared round a bend. Suddenly I felt really alone. Standing in that unfamiliar place, surrounded by acres of rolling countryside, I felt utterly insignificant and at the mercy of strangers. All through lunch, whenever I'd gazed out of the windows, I'd longed to explore but now I found I hadn't the heart to begin. There was no one to talk to. All the kids were on their beds and the staff were taking a brief, well-earned rest so I was definitely on my tod for an hour or two.

Leaning over the iron railings, I watched some brown-and-white sheep munching away at the short grass in their field. A ram with bedraggled wool and curly horns approached me aggressively, then turned away and began tearing at the grass again. For a few minutes I fantasized that the whole place belonged to me: the old house, the undulating fields with the sheep and goats – the lot. 'I'll have the pot-holes in the drive filled in next week,' I thought grandly. 'Then I'll clear out the stables and put horses back in there. Mine will be a white Arab mare and I'll ride her in the park every day.'

It was nice for a while but it's pretty boring to commune with yourself for long, so I scrambled over the railings and wandered up the field towards what appeared to be a high brick enclosure at the top. As I walked a lovely summery smell came up from the ground, a mixture of earth and grass and flowers all rolled into one. Looking back at the house nestling among the trees below my hillock, I was thrilled to see the lake I'd glimpsed when we arrived, glimmering softly under the bluest of skies. I love water so I almost dashed down the hill again, but first I wanted to find out what lay on the other side of the mysterious wall.

It was about three metres high and ran round four sides of a rectangle. The only entrance was a heavy door at one end and, lifting the latch, I tugged hard and darted inside. The door clicked behind me.

I found myself in the old kitchen garden. It was a rather sad place. Gnarled fruit trees bearing scabby apples and pears clung to the walls and a rotting greenhouse stretched along the east side. Half the garden was a neat vegetable patch growing all the usual things: carrots, peas, beans, etc. The other half was occupied by a dozen or so dusty brown chickens, pecking and scratching up the ground in their silly way. I began to wish I hadn't bothered after all but had gone straight down to the lake. Even so I like to know about places so I decided to have a look around before leaving.

Lifting the lid of the nesting boxes I discovered five eggs and a moth-eaten old hen stubbornly sitting on two others. She flapped and squawked indignantly when I shooed her off. Peeking inside the greenhouse I was amazed to find peaches and grapes flourishing in spite of the gaps in the glass; I promised myself I'd keep a greedy eye on them. There was really nothing more to see, so I headed for the door again and looked for the handle. Unbelievably, there wasn't one. I put my fingers through the hole where it should have been but could only feel the flaking paint on the outside of the door. Blindly I searched for the latch I had used when entering but, though it must have been there, I couldn't find it.

I did another tour of the garden hoping to discover an entrance hidden behind a fruit tree or the currant bushes. No luck, so I walked back again and in desperation I hurled myself at the door hoping it would burst open but I only succeeded in hurting my shoulder.

A familiar sick feeling started in the pit of my stomach and my stupid heart began to pound like it did before I was ill. Of course I knew immediately what it was. Fear. Dr Stobart had taught me to recognize the symptoms but they hadn't occurred for so long that I thought they had gone away. Unless I could exercise a measure of control I would soon start to sweat and shake and goodness knows what else. If it took a real hold I might have a relapse. The last thought pulled me together like a cold douche and, sinking down in the shadow of the wall, I deliberately let my mind go blank and my arms and legs flop as I had been taught. After all, I reasoned, there was plenty to eat in the garden so I wouldn't starve.

The heat was stifling. Not a breath of air stirred the serried rows of vegetables. Even the chickens seemed to be saving their energy for the cooler evening. Vaguely I wondered if I could climb a fruit tree and heave myself over the wall, but all the upper branches looked weak and even if I managed it without breaking them the top would still be out of reach. The sick feeling welled up again and to quell it I began to recite a poem I had studied with my tutor. It starts 'Glory be to God for dappled things . . . ' It's a calming, happy poem and I'd just said the last line when a dog barked outside and a voice shouted,

'Shut up, Plod, you idiot!'

For a moment I was so relieved that I just sat there like a dolt then I jumped up and yelled 'Hey! I'm stuck in here. Can you let me out?'

The dog started barking again like a hound of hell but the heavy door actually swung back and the boy I'd seen in the stable-yard came in followed by a young black labrador.

For a moment we stared at each other as we had, earlier, through my bedroom window.

'I — I was just exploring,' I stammered, suddenly conscious of my brief skirt and skinny top. Well, you are when someone else is in full working gear. You feel a bit silly.

He grinned. 'It's quite easy to get out. You've only got to pull the string on the outside of the door.'

I felt my face go scarlet. 'I didn't realize it was there.'

He shook his head in mock despair. 'Dear oh dear. That was a bit daft wasn't it? Suppose I hadn't come along. What then?'

I lifted my chin defiantly. 'I'd have shouted for help.'

'Oh yes? And who do you think would have heard you?'

'I dunno,' I said vaguely. 'Bill or Jane, I suppose.'

'This far from the house? The man in the moon as likely!'

'Anyway,' I protested spiritedly, 'if you are in charge of the garden you ought to fit a proper latch inside the door.'

His eyebrows disappeared under his swinging fringe. 'What for? No one ever gets stranded in here. Do you know why?'

'No, but . . .'

'Because,' he said amiably, 'it clearly states "Private" on the outside and most people can read.' He beckoned me over to see for myself.

'There's nothing clear about that,' I said indignantly. 'You ought to repaint it. It's a wonder the kids don't get trapped in here.'

'They've more sense,' he said. To cover my embarrassment I crouched down and made a fuss of the labrador, who licked my face with a long pink tongue. 'Good boy, Plod. Who does he belong to?'

'Me. By the way, what on earth have you been doing in here all this time?'

I looked up quickly. 'All this time?'

His face suddenly flushed a dull red and turning

away he stomped off in the direction of the chickens. I ran after him.

'All this time?' I repeated. 'You saw me go in, didn't you? You must have waited and waited thinking that any time I would probably yell for help and when I didn't curiosity got the better of you and along you came to see for yourself.'

He stopped in his tracks and gave a slightly shame-faced grin. 'Guilty m'lord as accused.'

I gasped. 'Why that's the rottenest thing . . '

He nodded. 'Pretty rotten, I agree, but I knew you wouldn't come to any harm and I thought it would teach you to look before you leap next time.'

I stared at him. Of course he didn't know I'd been ill and that being locked in anywhere stirred up all kinds of terrifying feelings. I must have gone all pale and glittery with anger because he suddenly looked wary and said, 'You *are* all right, aren' you?'

I'm not given to violence, not like my mum who'd go for Big Ben if it annoyed her, so I just stood there staring resentfully at him.

'You're not a – a guest or something are you?' he asked, displaying a sudden lack of confidence.

'I may be,' I said. 'I just may be a Very Important Guest and you may be in for a lot of trouble.'

'Then you'd be the first guest to be given that room over the stables,' he said, laughing; and he walked on towards the chickens.

I let him go. 'If you want to know, I'm Nell Carter,' I called after him. 'I've come to help out for a few weeks.'

He turned and walked back. 'That's nice. I'm Jim Blair and I don't help out, I work, so I don't have much

27

time to stand around.' He lifted a hand. 'See you. Come along, Plod.'

But Plod, sensing a new and willing playmate, left the hole he was digging, bounded over to me and stood quivering with anticipation. I picked up a stick and threw it along the path. He chased after it.

'Plod!' Jim called roughly but the dog ignored him.

Laughing inwardly I strolled towards the door, followed by an eager Plod, stick in mouth. At the exit I turned. 'If you are collecting the eggs,' I said sweetly, 'it might interest you to know that you've got a broody hen.' And swinging round I left the garden with the dog leaping excitedly around me.

Taking the stick from him I hurled it far down the meadow and watched him race after it, then I ran down the slope through the buttercups and daisies. The sun felt hot on my bare shoulders and the whole countryside was bursting with the honey sweetness of a July day. Leaping the railings I headed for the lake and firmly thrust Jim Blair to the back of my mind. Or tried to.

Chapter 5

The work at Finchings was so concentrated and so different from anything I'd done before that I often felt like giving up. I don't think I'd have lasted a week if it hadn't been for Marion Glease. Fortunately she was the first person I met on Monday morning. We collided on the stairs, I and this tall gangling girl with bushy black hair and a toothy grin.

'Hi! You must be the rookie,' she said.

'Right,' I groaned, rubbing the ankle she'd managed to kick.

'I'm Marion.'

'I'm Nell.'

'Come on, then, or we'll be late.' She bounded down the stairs ahead of me. 'We have to manage Monday breakfast on our own because Jane and Bill are doing other things.'

Before long I was busy spooning Bran Buds into open mouths and mopping up spilt milk. The noise was indescribable and some of the kids became quite truculent if they had to wait too long for their grub. To me it seemed utter chaos but Marion was great: calm, dryly joky and amazingly efficient. The kids obviously respected and trusted her and they obeyed her without question. I learned a lot from Marion that first morning.

After breakfast we had the loo parade and I'd better gloss over that bit because, to be truthful, it wasn't very nice. Some of them had no control and had to wear sort of nappy things, which is okay on an infant but definitely yukky on an older kid. That part of the job took some getting used to, I can tell you. Marion did all the dirty work while I stood around like a lemon, just watching.

'Revolting, isn't it?' she said cheerfully when the operation was over and we were scrubbing up at the sink. 'Never mind, just think of them as babies, because that's what some of them are really. They respond to food and warmth and love and laughter and a firm hand. They need stimulating, too. That's the most interesting bit.'

She sounded so experienced.

'How long have you been working here?' I asked.

'Since I was thirteen. That makes four years now. I used to come during school holidays and weekends but when I finally left school Jane and Bill took me on full time.'

'Do you live at home?'

'Yeah. Mum takes in PGs during the summer, so I help her out as much as I can.'

'Do you think you'll stay here or move on and do something else?'

She seemed surprised. 'What sort of thing?'

'I dunno. Be a hairdresser or a secretary or something?'

'Oh, that sort of thing. No. I like the kids, and Jane and Bill treat me very fairly. Finchings has got me for life — or anyway until I get married.' She gave a sheepish grin. 'That's if anyone ever wants to marry me.'

'Of course they will,' I said stoutly. I could already tell, from the way she stooped and allowed her hair to fall across her face, that she had a mammoth complex about her height and looks. Silly really, because she had big brown eyes and a lively face and was vivacious and attractive. But from the way she spoke I guessed she hadn't had much luck with her love life. Nor had I, come to that, but the last three years had been so taken up with my relationship with Mark that I hadn't given too much thought to boys.

'I don't want to get married for ages,' I said.

'Have you got a steady boyfriend?' she asked, curiosity flickering in her brown eyes.

An unexpected and terrible sense of loss suddenly swept through me.

'I had,' I said sadly, 'but he got engaged to someone else.' I really hadn't meant to lie but I'd always thought of Mark as my boyfriend so the words just slipped out before I could stop them.

Her expressive eyes filled with sympathy. 'That's awful.'

Fishing in the back pocket of my jeans I pulled out the crumpled photograph I always carried with me.

'That was taken last summer.'

'He's terribly good-looking,' she said. 'How old is he?'

'Twenty-seven.'

She looked impressed.

'He had to marry money in the end,' I said casually. 'His parents insisted.'

She whistled through her teeth. 'That must have been rotten for you.'

'Yeah.' My eyes filled with angry tears. 'She may be rich but he doesn't love her really. He loves me.' Blinking away the tears, I straightened the roller-towel. 'Anyway, I'd rather not talk aboout it if you don't mind.'

As we shepherded the kids outside to play, I couldn't help wondering why I'd said all that. It had been sort of satisfying to see her getting more and more intrigued so I'd just gone on, building on the first lie. Now I'd never be able to retract. Not that it mattered. After all, Mark had definitely gone out of my life. Anyway, it had been lovely to talk about him to someone who was interested. Lovely but painful. Oh Mark . . .

The first week passed in a haze of activity. There was so much to do. From seven in the morning, when I assisted the night staff to get the children up and change their (often filthy) beds, until eight in the evening, when they were all in bed again, I hardly had a moment to myself. In the beginning I fell into my own bed every night, too tired to think, wondering how I'd managed to get myself into such a situation. Gradually, however, things sorted themselves out and I began to know the children, not just by their various disabilities but as individuals – personalities in their own right.

Take Rachel, for example, whom I'd met on my first day, she had seemed such a bright happy child then, but I sometimes found her in odd corners of the house, crying as though her little heart would break. No one knew why (I don't think she knew herself) but when I put my arms around her and sang her a snatch of Stevie Wonder's latest she soon cheered up and laughed and jigged around to the music.

Some of the kids had infantile minds and were unable to communicate their needs properly, but after a while I became adept at spotting trouble a mile off. You had to, because without the kind of sixth sense that warned you when something was wrong, you were lost. One morning, before I was fully tuned in, I was helping three kids with their finger painting in the big playroom when I heard a crash and a yell and whipping round I saw that seven-year-old Ben had stuck his fist right through a window-pane because five-year-old Rory was standing outside making faces at him. Ben was rushed to the doctor, who put four stitches in his wrist, after which he recovered with remarkable speed. I fully expected to get the sack but Jane and Bill were sympathetic and understanding.

'I know it's difficult, but you mustn't get so involved with individuals that you don't know what the rest are doing,' was about the only comment Jane made.

I promised I wouldn't.

Jane and Bill completely justified my first impression of them. Jane never indulged in idle chat, and as everything she said was to the point you always knew what she expected of you. She was good at listening, too. I could take a problem to her at any moment of the day and she would stop what she was doing to give it her full attention. Although she could be sharp she was never moody and I always felt she regarded me as a person and not just as an extra pair of hands.

Bill was different. He never relaxed but was always rushing about like a blue-arsed fly (Dad's expression, not mine) fixing this and that and talking non-stop. He did most of the cooking – aided by Jean from the village – and was as moody and temperamental as a Master Chef. This made me a bit wary of him, but I soon learned to sense his moods and approach him accordingly. After all, I'd done it with Mum for years.

Marion was the mainstay of my life. The more I got to know her the more I liked her and the more laughs we had. When I'd been at Finchings for about ten days she invited me to visit her family on my day off. I told Bill and Jane about the invitation that evening at supper.

Jane nodded approvingly. 'I'm so glad you and Marion have hit it off. She's really nice. I don't know what we'd do without her.'

'Pity about the brothers,' Bill said.

'What about them?' I asked.

'One is out of work,' Jane said. 'In fact I don't think he's worked since he left school. But that's hardly his fault.'

Bill raised an eyebrow. 'Isn't it? The local paper is

full of boring or dirty jobs. When we wanted the pot-holes in the drive filled in we put it around the Youth Club to see if anyone was interested. Were they, hell! My guess is that Master Glease prefers the dole queue to working for a living. The younger brother is just as bad.'

'Oh come along, Bill!' Jane protested. 'Be fair. Nick Glease had an accident that ruined his chances of becoming a career footballer. That's the equivalent of being a film star in our day. The boy will get over it. Just give him time.'

'What happened?' I asked, as Bill and I collected up the soup plates and transferred the cold chicken and salad to the table. Jane stayed put in her chair. She was like that – a bundle of energy in the day and as limp as a wilted lettuce leaf when all the kids were safely in bed.

'Nick Glease was always very nimble on his feet,' she mused, while Bill whisked the salad with the air of a professional. 'Even as a toddler he seemed to get around faster than other children of his age. His father – a fanatic amateur footballer – soon spotted it and gave the child a football when he was three. Nick kicked it around all the time and Ted became very excited about the boy's natural aptitude. (By the way, I got all this from Mrs Glease, who used to work for us before she started taking PGs.) Of course all his friends thought Ted was crazy but he stuck to his guns. "One day my boy will be as famous as George Best," he would say, ignoring the taunts and jibes. Well, his confidence paid off because as young Nick grew up the talent scouts began to come around and finally the Football Association showed definite interest. Then last year Nick was selected to train at the FA's new school, at Lilleshall in Shropshire, along with the cream of the country's young hopefuls. In fact, he was due to take up his place there this September.'

She stopped speaking.

'Well,' I asked impatiently. 'What happened?'

'Ted Glease died of a heart attack while he and Nick were out training,' she said grimly. 'That's what happened.'

I gasped. 'Poor Nick.'

'Poor everyone. As you can imagine, the whole family were very cut up. Mrs Glease went around looking like death warmed up for months. Marion, poor love, felt it as much as anyone but had to carry everything on her young shoulders. Dan, the elder brother, was certainly no help and Nick climbed on to the school roof for a dare, fell off and fractured both legs in four places.'

'No more football?'

'Well, no Lilleshall, anyway. I'm afraid George Best's reputation will never be challenged by Nick Glease. He is still not walking properly.'

'It must be difficult for him at school after all that,' I said feelingly.

Bill snorted. 'He hasn't got the guts to go back.'

'Bill, you are being very unfair,' Jane said. 'I'm sure the boy will be back when he is fit.'

'The Education Authority deemed him fit three months ago,' Bill said. 'If he fails to turn up this term they've threatened to send him to a special school. The accident was entirely the boy's own fault. Everyone has been extremely tolerant.'

Jane glared at him. 'You are such a blimp! You completely underestimate the effect Ted Glease's death had on the family. He was a tremendously strong personality. When he died so suddenly they didn't know what had hit them. I don't understand why Nick can't be given a home tutor until he feels like facing everyone again. After all, other Education Authorities do it, why can't ours?'

'Home tutor!' Bill scoffed. 'That's a mighty soft option if ever I heard one. No wonder the bill for education is so exorbitant. That boy should return to school where he would be given all the help he needs.' He shook his head, leaving us in no doubt about his attitude to the matter.

My stomach was tying itself into knots during this conversation. If Bill despised the home tutor system so much I'd better not reveal my own chequered education. In fact it would be wise to duck all questions about it. Having just begun to enjoy myself at Finchings, I certainly didn't want to fall foul of Bill because Nick Glease and I had a common hang-up about going back to school.

Jane must have sensed my uneasiness because she smiled reassuringly and said, 'Bill's not really the old bear he makes out. It's just that most of the kids here will never be able to take advantage of an education that everyone else takes for granted and it makes him mad when someone deliberately throws away their chances.'

I nodded and popped a large piece of bread into my mouth so I wouldn't have to speak. Life, it seemed, was full of traps and I'd just avoided walking right into one. It was enough to make a person quite nervous.

Chapter 6

The sun was blazing through my window when I awoke the next morning, and for a while I just lay there luxuriating in the knowledge that I could linger instead of tearing over to the house to help with the kids and the smelly beds. Then I got up, raked through my cupboard and decided to wear my new baggy pink dungarees. I put a scarlet plastic clip on one side of my head and a string of scarlet beads around my neck, collected up my swimming gear, towel and beach bag, then went over to the kitchen. Everyone else was busy working, so I had the place to myself for once. Peace. I was rapidly discovering that you don't miss it until you don't have it. Anyway, after a blissful solitary breakfast and a leisurely glance through the funnies in the papers I ambled down the drive to the bus stop.

Apparently if you missed the bus you had to wait an hour for another one. Well, I missed it. One cup of coffee too many, I thought, staring ruefully after its retreating back. The question was, should I walk the three miles into town, hitch a lift, or go home and wait for the next one? While I was thus deliberating an old pick-up truck stopped in front of me and Jim Blair stuck his head out of the window.

'Missed the bus, have you?' he said, grinning like a fool.

'Oh no,' I said sarcastically, 'I came specially to

watch it trundle by. I'm a bus-spotter. Didn't you know?'

'Then you won't be wanting a lift will you?'

'A lift?' I looked the vehicle over disdainfully. 'In that old thing? I thought you must be on your way to the knacker's with it.'

'If you want to come, get in,' he said and drew back into the cab.

Of course I did. I hadn't much option. As I slammed the rotten old door I wondered why Jim Blair always made me feel a bit nervous. I hadn't seen much of him since our encounter in the vegetable garden but whenever we met I had the idea that he was quietly laughing at me because of the fool I'd made of myself that day.

'Your day off?' he asked as we bumped downhill towards the town.

'Yup.'

'Thought so. You look all togged up.'

'What, these old things?' I said, casually brushing a speck of dirt off my new dungarees.

'Well, you usually wear jeans, don't you?'

So he'd noticed what I wore. Wonders would never cease. Jim Blair had the reputation of avoiding girls like the plague. Marion and the others thought he was attractive in a smouldering sort of way, but shy and a bit thick. They were wrong. I'd seen the gleam in his eyes under the swinging fringe of hair and if Jim was thick I was little Miss Muffet. As for being attractive, well I could see what they meant but I still dreamt about Mark every night and I seriously doubted if any male would ever be able to stir my heart again.

'What are you going to do in town?' he asked.

'Marion Glease has asked me to lunch but I'm a bit

early, so I thought I'd have a swim or look around the shops or something.'

'I've got to do some shopping,' he said. 'Matter of fact I need a bit of help if you've nothing better to do.'

Not exactly graciously put but I couldn't very well refuse as he'd given me a lift.

'What is it?' I asked.

'I've got to buy my dad a birthday present.'

I groaned inwardly. I'd suffered enough from Dad's inability to choose a present for Mum. The hours we'd spent staggering from shop to shop in search of the perfect gift would have enabled us to read the Encyclopaedia Britannica through twice.

Jim parked in the multi-storey and we walked through an alley into the main shopping street. The heat in town was far fiercer than in the country and I longed to be off to the beach for a swim. To be truthful, I was beginning to resent Jim's dad's birthday quite a bit.

'What do you plan to get him?' I asked, forcing myself to show an interest.

'What do you think about a pair of slippers?'

'Boring.'

'Really? I thought girls liked clothes.'

'Slippers aren't clothes. They're just coverings for the feet. Why don't you give him a bright sweater or something?'

'Because he'd leave it in his drawer and wear his old one.'

'What about a good book?'

'He only reads agricultural catalogues.'

'A bottle of booze, then?'

'He makes his own wine.'

'Well if he doesn't read and he doesn't drink what does he do?' By this time I sounded as exasperated as I felt. The heat eddied round us in small dusty blasts until your hair was a mess and your eyes felt gritty.

'He gardens a bit, then after gardening he comes in and puts on his slippers – which are now worn out.'

'Then I suppose we'd better get him some,' I said wearily.

Taking my elbow he piloted me inside a shoe shop. 'The thing is I need your help over the colour. I'm not too good at colour but you're okay, judging from your clothes.'

Hm. So he'd definitely had his eye on me. Interesting.

I chose cheerful red slippers. They were leather and rather expensive.

'I hope he likes them,' I said anxiously when we left the shop. 'Suppose he just leaves them in the box?'

'Then he'll have to go barefoot,' Jim said calmly, 'because I burnt his old ones this morning.'

I looked at him with amazement. 'Won't he mind?'

He shrugged. 'When two people live together there's a limit to endurance. They stank.'

I collapsed laughing, in fact we both did. When we'd recovered we went into a café and ordered two coffee ice-creams which arrived in cut-glass dishes with twirly wafers sticking out of the middle. Jim paid for them.

'Do you and your dad get along okay?' I asked, savouring the cool sweet taste of the ice-cream.

'We have to. We're in business together. Plant hire. Diggers, tractors, hedge-cutting – that kind of thing. We're very busy now with the harvest.'

'But I thought you worked for Bill and Jane.'

He laughed. 'No way. Our cottage is in their

grounds and they inherited us as sitting tenants. They've always been very fair, so I help them out as much as possible.'

'Jim Blair!' I pointed my ice-cream spoon accusingly at him. 'You *were* helping them out the day we met in the kitchen garden!'

He had the grace to blush and grin and look a bit shamefaced.

'Okay, but you were standing there looking so pleased with yourself . . .'

'Pleased with myself?' I yelped. 'I was really scared in there. How could you . . ?'

He raised a pacifying hand. 'Okay. Okay. I did wrong. I'm sorry. Now could we forget it and start all over again?'

'Okay,' I said slowly. 'If you promise not to do anything like that again.'

'I promise.'

We stared at each other. It was as if we'd made some kind of pact that had nothing to do with the episode in the garden. Matter of fact I didn't know what it had to do with, I only know it was made and afterwards it felt as though we'd known each other for years.

Jim glanced at his watch. 'Well, I suppose I'd better be getting back. That's one thing about working for yourself — there's no one to give you the sack if you take a long lunch-break.'

He dropped me outside Marion's house and I watched him drive away. I liked him better than before, no doubt about that, but he had a disconcerting way of looking at you as though he knew you better than you knew yourself. Silly really; I mean no one can know you better than you, can they?

Marion was painting her nails in her bedroom, her

tape-recorder going at full blast, so I had to wait until the music stopped before telling her about Jim.

'He knew he was going to buy his dad slippers all the time,' I said, 'so I can't think why he wanted me to go with him.'

Marion screwed the top on to the polish. 'Kid, you've made history,' she said grinning. 'Jim Blair fancies you.'

'You must be joking.'

She peered at herself in the mirror. 'I'm not. I wish someone fancied me. Someone fanciable – not just that wimp across the street who makes eyes at me all the time.'

'Someone will,' I said. 'It'll happen when you least expect it – or so they say.'

'Across a crowded room I suppose?'

I giggled. 'Across a crowded bus more likely.'

'P'raps I'm just not trendy enough. My clothes and that.'

It was on the tip of my tongue to agree with her – she dressed like someone twice her age – but I thought better of it. After all, the Gleases had had a lousy year with one thing and another and they were probably short of the ready. I knew Marion handed over most of her pay packet to her Mum, so there couldn't be much left over for clothes. Anyway, I wasn't at all sure that her clothes were to blame. It could have been the oddly eager yet hangdog air she wore whenever boys were around – even the wimp across the street. It was as though she was saying 'Notice me. Notice me,' but at the same time expecting to be kicked out of the way like a stray dog no one wanted.

'P'raps I should dye my hair or something,' she said, tugging at her bushy locks.

I studied her worried reflection. 'It might give you a bit of a lift I suppose.'

'You sound doubtful.'

'Well, what if it looked awful?

She nodded gloomily. 'Yeah. What if it did?'

I knew she needed to be cheered up so I grabbed her arm and yanked her to her feet. 'Let's go to Boots and look at their range of hair tints, then if we see something fantastic we'll buy it and have a go.'

Her face broke into a delighted grin. 'You're a pal, Nell. I'm so glad you came to Finchings.'

That made me feel really good because all my friendships had faded when I dropped out of school and although I now regretted it I didn't know how to pick them up again. You can't just get on the blower and burble 'Hi, Sally, I know I haven't been in touch for three years but I'm ready to be friends again.' So you see a new friend was a big (and I mean big) event in my life.

We decided to have lunch before going to Boots, and when we went down to the kitchen I saw that a boy was already sitting at the table. A couple of sticks were hooked over the back of his chair.

'Nick, this is Nell,' Marion said as we sat down. Nick turned a pair of wary hazel eyes in my direction and nodded briefly. He was thin and pale, as though he never left the house, and his mouth was set in a sulky, obstinate expression.

'Hi,' I said cheerily. 'I've heard a lot about you, Nick.'

His top lip curled unpleasantly. 'Yeah. I bet.'

Mrs Glease saved the day by bustling across the room with a plate of toad-in-the-hole and peas, which she plonked in front of me.

'I know it's a bit hot for sausages, Nell, but they just had to be eaten up.'

'They look good,' I said – truthfully as it happens.

She beamed with pleasure. 'My lot love sausages even in the hottest weather.'

She was nice and homely with frizzy brown hair, pink cheeks and lively eyes. If I hadn't known that she'd recently been widowed I'd never have guessed. She seemed so bright and sparkey. In spite of the sulky Nick they gave the impression of a close-knit family and although I was enjoying myself I was aware of a faintly jealous feeling. Why hadn't I been born into such a family?

Mrs Glease's voice cut into my thoughts. 'Marion really enjoys working with the kids at Finchings. I'm glad she's doing something worthwhile instead of standing round some daft boutique looking bored. I expect your mother feels the same.'

There was an awkward pause while I chomped on a sausage, then I said, 'Mum's dead. It was a car accident three years ago.'

A shocked silence gripped everyone at the table. Even Nick stopped eating, with his fork half-way to his mouth. I chomped on as if I hadn't noticed their stunned reaction.

'Oh you poor dear,' Mrs Glease breathed, putting her hand on her heart. 'We all know exactly how you feel. My Ted's death affected us very badly. I expect Marion told you about it. Do you have any brothers or sisters?'

I shook my head. 'No. Dad and I live alone now. It's okay. We manage.'

She nodded understandingly. 'Yes. Life must go on

after all but it's nothing short of tragic. A home without a father is one thing but without a mother . . . '

I gave a sad little smile. 'Yeah. Well . . .'

'You must treat this as home while you're here,' she said firmly. 'Now promise me you will.'

'Thanks. I mean, that's really kind.'

'That means you'll have to do your turn at the washing up,' Marion said grinning.

Nick didn't say anything but he gave me the last sausage on the dish — a gesture that spoke louder than words.

Well, I'd done it again, hadn't I? And this time it had been a much bigger whopper than the one I'd told Marion about Mark being my boyfriend. It was getting to be a habit, and one I felt distinctly uneasy about. I used to lie to Mum quite a bit to save myself from the consequences of her rotten temper, so it had been easy enough to slip into the groove again. And, though I didn't like doing it, neither did I fancy going into details about her bolt for freedom — or whatever it was. Death was at least final — it was doubtful if anyone would mention her again — whereas a defecting mother could be a recurring embarrassment.

After lunch Nick surprisingly asked me to play draughts with him.

'Go on,' Marion said. 'He's bored with beating Mum and me all the time.

So, while Marion and Mrs G. washed the dishes and prepared tea for the PGs, Nick and I faced each other across the draughts board. He had the killer instinct, I'll say that for him, but I'd played board games for therapy during my illness, so I was a formidable opponent. At first he resented being beaten but I cheerfully ignored his sulks and eventually he took a couple of games off me, which miraculously restored him to a good humour.

'You're more fun to play with than Marion or Mum,' he admitted grudgingly. 'They don't concentrate.'

'You'd probably get a better game with your mates at school,' I said casually.

He was setting out the pieces as I spoke and I saw his thin shoulders suddenly tighten and hunch over the board.

'I don't go to school at the moment,' he said.

I placed my last man in position. 'Oh? Why not?'

'It's my legs. I'm not walking properly yet.'

I nodded sympathetically, though I'd watched him cross to the cupboard to get out the draughts without using his stick at all. He hadn't looked exactly like a marathon walker but he'd managed to get there and back unaided, so what Bill had suggested was true: Nick could have gone back to school if he'd wanted. He didn't want and I wondered why.

I made the first move. 'Does the school send you stuff to do at home?'

'Yeah. Our neighbour was a teacher, so she helped me a bit, but she's moved away and now there's no one.'

'It must be so boring.'

'Yeah.'

'When are they going to let you go back?'

'Dunno.'

'You were walking pretty well a few moments ago.'

'No I wasn't. I broke both legs.' He looked up proudly. 'In four places.'

'Yeah, I heard.'

'It's a wonder I'm not a cripple for life.' He whisked away a couple of my men. 'You're not concentrating.'

I tried another tack. 'You must have been sick as a cat about missing out on Lilleshall.'

Suddenly he slammed his fist down on the board, scattering the draughts right, left and centre. 'I don't want to talk about that!'

'All right. All right. Keep your shirt on.' I admit it had been pretty heavy-footed of me to jump in like that.

Getting up, I wandered over to the window and raised the net curtain. The grass in the small front garden was brown from the heat and a few miserable roses struggled in their final death throes in front of the yellowing privet hedge. A few kids were kicking a ball up and down the road, dodging to the pavement if a car came along. An ever-present reminder of now unattainable glories for Nick who, no doubt, used to be the star of the group. It was my fault he'd exploded. I'd dug too deep. Stupid.

Of course if I hadn't fibbed about Mum I could have told him my own story which might, just might, have helped him. Not that someone else's troubles cure your own but they do at least show you're not the only pebble on the beach. Anyway, I reasoned guiltily, if I had been able to tell him about myself it wouldn't have been much use because, when all was said and done, we were two of a kind — perfectly able to return to school but determined, for our own reasons, to stay away.

I let the net curtain slide slowly out of my fingers, wondering how I'd had the gall to question Nick at all as I was obviously the worst possible person to do so.

Chapter 7

Turning back into the room I began to gather up the
scattered draughts, conscious of Nick, slumped on his
chair, watching me moodily. Suddenly the front door
slammed and a voice called 'Anything to eat, Mum?
I'm starved!'

After some muffled conversation in the kitchen, the
sitting-room door was flung open and a boy of about
eighteen stood on the threshold. He was good-looking
with wavy, slicked-back brown hair and sparkey hazel
eyes. He didn't look like Marion or Mrs Glease but he
bore a distinct resemblance to Nick. In fact he was a
more robust version of his brother, but thicker-set and
with a cock-of-the-walk air that the younger boy
lacked. Swaggering into the room he roughly tousled
Nick's hair.

'Had another fit of tantrums, little brother?'

'Ger out of it!' growled Nick, and grabbing his stick
he limped laboriously from the room.

'I'm Dan,' the boy said, grinning at my red-faced
attempts to recover a draught from under the sofa.

'Hi,' I said shortly. 'Instead of just standing there
you can help me find these things. There's one by your
foot.' I mean he'd really annoyed me by provoking
Nick like that. And I'd have bet a penny to a pound he
did it all the time. A great way to encourage Nick to get
himself together again.

He shrugged. 'I don't mind helping a pretty girl once in a while.' And dropping to a squatting position he continued to stare at me until I felt myself getting quite hot and bothered. It was downright embarrassing. A person ought not to do that when he first meets you. He was even better-looking than Mark, bursting with life and pent-up energy. So much so that you wondered if he might suddenly go beserk and start leap-frogging over the furniture or something. It's difficult to describe his effect on me; I only know that I felt drawn to him, as if he was some kind of a magnet. He wore a crimson T-shirt with a black gilet and black jeans and had a massive digital watch clamped to his wrist.

'So you're Nell and you work in that loony bin with Marion.'

I bridled indignantly. 'It's not a loony bin.'

He gave a hoot of laughter. 'You're as easy to get a rise out of as she is.'

'Oh well, as long as it amuses you . . .' Tossing the last draught into the box I clapped on the lid and stood up. He wasn't much taller than I but he had broad shoulders and muscular arms and legs. He, not Nick, should have been the footballer, I thought, looking around for somewhere to park the draughts box.

Without shifting his gaze from my face he took the box and dropped it on to a table. 'You're much too pretty to frown like that,' he said in a low sexy voice.

I immediately giggled and before I knew what was happening he had grabbed me and was kissing me like there was no tomorrow – right there in his Mum's sitting room. I kept casting frantic looks over his shoulder at the door. The potential embarrassment was too awful to contemplate. Finally he let me go and I fell back slightly stunned but before I had time to gather my wits he seized my hand and dragged me into the hall.

'I'm just taking Nell for a ride on the bike,' he called, unhooking a couple of helmets from the hall-stand and giving one to me.

Minutes later we were zooming along the sea front, me with my hands firmly locked around Dan's waist in case I fell off. I'd never ridden pillion and it was unnerving to find oneself rocketing along, narrowly missing buses, bikes, prams, pedestrians; swaying to the right, swaying to the left, whizzing round corners, tearing through quiet streets, scattering dogs and kids in all directions. At last we slowed down and finally stopped near a shelter on the promenade.

We took off our helmets and sank on to the shelter seat. The blood was racing in my veins and my skin tingled from the wind. I felt incredibly alive and powerful. The sea looked blue and inviting for once, with little white crests nipping about all over the glittering surface. Kids and adults of all ages were bobbing about in the water or kicking balls or throwing stones for barking dogs. It looked like a toy scene and it seemed to me, all powerful as I was, that I could alter anything I wanted by simply focusing my gaze on my subject. I was so fascinated by this thought that I was only aware Dan had asked a question when he poked me in the ribs.

'What?'

He laughed. 'Dreamer! I said did you enjoy the ride?'

'Sure – after the first couple of minutes.'

'Most girls would have been scared stiff.'

'That so?'

'Yeah. You've got guts. I really put the bike through

its paces.' His hand closed over mine but I remained totally unresponsive. Enough's enough when you've only just met a guy; specially when nothing like it has happened to you before.

'Nell . . .' He cleared his throat. 'Have you got a . . .I mean is there a guy . . . you know . . . at the moment?'

'N-not exactly,' I stuttered.

'What do you mean?'

'I mean no, there isn't.'

'So can I see you sometimes – take you out on the bike and that?'

'Why not?' Although I sounded casual my heart was thumping wildly. Could this really be happening to me?

'Great.' He turned the full force of his sexy grin on me, then I was suddenly in his arms again and he was kissing me like crazy and I was kissing him back. This went on until his hands started to wander, at which point I shoved him away.

'Hey, none of that!'

He laughed. 'Okay, but a little of what you fancy does you good, they say.'

'Oh do they? Well, I've had the little I fancy so let's get out of here.' And I leapt to my feet.

As we put on our helmets he said, 'Must stop for some fags on the way home.'

After another dash through the town we drew up outside a tobacconist.

Dan patted his pockets. 'Heck! I've left my cash in my other jacket. Have you got any?'

'Sure.' I fished out a couple of quid.

When he came out of the shop he gave me the change. 'Thanks, Nell. I'll pay you back.'

Marion looked a bit sour when we walked in and I can't say I blamed her. After all I'd been invited to spend the day with her, not with Dan.

'It's too late to go to Boots for hair-colour if we want to make the cinema on time,' she complained.

'Sorry, Marion,' I said guiltily.

Dan hung up the helmets and joined us in the kitchen. 'Did I hear cinema? What are you going to see?'

Marion gave him a dirty look. 'Whatever's on. And you're not coming either because I'm not paying for you.'

'That's okay,' he said cheerfully. 'Mum will lend me the money.'

'Oh he is awful!' Marion fumed when he'd gone. 'He's always getting money out of Mum. Make sure you never lend him any.'

'He wouldn't ask me,' I said lightly.

She gave a humourless little laugh. 'Don't be too sure. He'd con his own shadow, Dan would.'

But I knew that already and quite frankly I didn't care.

In the cinema I made sure that Marion sat between Dan and me. Something told me he might not keep his hands to himself and I certainly didn't want to antagonize Marion more than I'd done already. The film was Mel Brooks at his zaniest so we all had a good laugh, then went back to supper. Afterwards I said I'd better be getting back to Finchings and Dan and Marion had an argument about whether I should go on the bus or the bike.

'It's a good five miles,' Marion said. 'She'll get blown to bits.'

'Nonsense, she'll love it,' Dan said. 'I'll lend her some windproof gear.'

'Yours will be too large,' Nick chimed in. 'I'll lend her something of mine.'

By this time I felt like a parcel ready to be wrapped and posted. Not that I minded. It was nice being the centre of attention for once. Anyway, in the end I borrowed some goggles and a warm jacket and we covered the five miles in little more than five minutes.

When we turned into the drive Dan stopped the bike and got off.

'Not in a hurry are you?'

'Well . . .' I glanced at my watch. It was nine-thirty. 'I'd better not be late.'

'We've got time for a fag, haven't we?'

'You mean you have. I don't smoke.'

'So I've noticed. What are you afraid of – cancer or something?'

'Yeah. And bronchitis. And heart disease. You know, little things like that.'

He propped up the bike and we wandered off the drive and sat on the grass under a massive leafy tree. Dan put an arm round my shoulders. I felt a teeny bit uneasy. Perhaps I should have gone straight into the house and not fallen for this 'just time for a fag' routine.

'Relax,' he said in my left ear. 'Your shoulders feel like the back of a well-made chair.'

I shifted uncomfortably. 'I thought you were going to have a cigarette.'

'Okay, okay.' He dropped his arm, got out a fag and lit it.

'We'll just talk,' he said. 'You can ask me all about me.'

'Why should I want to know all about you?'

He grinned. 'Most girls want to know all about me. It's my animal magnetism, I guess.'

'You're the most conceited person I've ever met,' I said laughing.

'You mean you don't find me irresistible?'

'I certainly don't but . . .' I hesitated then went boldly on. 'There is something I'd like to know.'

'What did I tell you!' He said triumphantly.

'Do you mind being out of work?'

'Oh that. Well I get a bit bored and it would be great to have more cash but, on the whole, no. Why?'

I shrugged. 'Just curious.'

'I did enough work at school. And where has it got me? I'm having a nice long holiday now. I suppose I'll get down to it – to something – some day. I don't know what, though.'

'Aren't you interested in anything special?'

'Yeah.' The arm crept round my shoulders again. 'Pretty chicks.'

'No, Dan, I'm serious.'

'Then don't be. God, you sound like my mum.'

'Well, you said I could ask.'

'Look at it this way. Unemployment's never been higher. Millions of people would sell their grannies for a job. Isn't it lucky that guys like me are happy to stay out of the race.'

'But what do you do all day?'

'Oh I get around,' he said vaguely. 'Meet my mates, tease my little brother – that kind of thing.'

'Doesn't sound much fun.'

'Look,' his voice took on a raspy edge. 'Everyone's always lecturing me about getting a job. I get really pissed off with it.'

'Pissed off? That's lovely, that is.'

'Got delicate eardrums have you?'

'You could say.'

'I'll try to remember and just you remember to keep off the subject of jobs.'

There was an awkward silence, then I looked at my watch again. 'Well, thanks for the lift. I'd better go in now.'

He twisted me round to face him. 'See you Saturday? You do want to see me again, don't you?'

'I — I guess so,' I mumbled uncertainly. He really had me so confused I didn't know what I wanted. By this time our noses were touching and we were squinting into each other's eyes.

'Of course you do,' he murmured, his lips against my lips. 'And I want to see you, so . . .' The rest of the sentence was lost in a long searching kiss during which I somehow found myself spread-eagled on the grass with Dan on top of me.

'Hey, get off!' I said and shoved him hard in the chest, which sent him rolling away from me. In a flash I was on my feet and backing down the drive.

'Bye Dan. See you Saturday.'

'Wait! Don't you want a ride?'

'No thanks. I'd rather walk.'

He shrugged and walking over to the bike kicked away the prop, pulled on his helmet and disappeared in a cloud of dust and fumes.

When he'd gone I turned around and began to walk up the drive. A hundred metres ahead of me a solitary figure was also plodding towards the house. It looked like . . . yes, it definitely was Jim Blair. He must have passed right by as we were merrily snogging away in the grass. Not that it mattered. Much. Unless of course he let it slip to Bill or Jane. They wouldn't be too keen on an employee blatantly fooling around with a boy they strongly disapproved of, in their grounds, in full view of all passers-by. They might reach the reluctant conclusion that she wasn't very responsible. Or worse. By the time I reached the house Jim had disappeared but I resolved to have it out with him soon.

Chapter 8

The next few days were busier than usual. Rachel – my favourite although I'd never have admitted it – fell ill. She'd been clingy and listless for a couple of days so Jane called in the doctor. He couldn't find much wrong but the next day she developed a temperature, so we removed her to the 'hospital' room and began a course of antibiotics. Because Rachel was lonely and fretted for her friends, Jane took me off my other duties and asked me to stay with her until she improved.

The pills worked quickly but Rachel had to stay in bed and it was hard work entertaining her and keeping her happy. There were times when I could have yelled with frustration but there were rewarding times, too, when she seemed to grow in understanding and responsiveness. Often, I'm afraid, it was very boring. Caring for a handicapped kid from dawn to dusk may be regarded as a challenge but, in my opinion, half the challenge lies in fighting off the yawns. I began to get an inkling of what it must be like to be the mother of a child like Rachel. However much you loved her, you must often want to pack her off somewhere and forget her for a while. Then, of course, you'd feel guilty and kick yourself for being so rotten. No wonder people were glad of places like Finchings. I mean we were probably saving the marriages – the sanity, even – of some parents.

Sometimes Rachel dropped off for half an hour and I'd make for the garden and jog around to get rid of some of my energy. Sometimes I would just sit by the open window and dream. The fantastic weather continued. The lawns were burnt brown and we were short of water, which created problems with the children, but I never heard anyone complain.

I used to wonder if they were having the same weather at home and how Dad was coping on his own. This often led me to thinking about Mum and Dad, and Mum's bunk and my illness but, for the first time, my thoughts did not turn into a series of sharp, hurtful images. Instead they were calm and reflective. Over and over again I recalled how M and D had been with each other. Like incompatible strangers locked in an empty carriage on an endless train journey. I remembered the atmosphere of nervy frustration generated by Mum, and Dad's stolid refusal to be affected by it. I was affected though. The mere sight of her tight lips and drooping fag when I got home from school was enough to bring me out in a prickly sweat. Thinking about it now I wondered if my breakdown was more the result of the angry years before Mum disappeared than the gap left by her actual departure.

Poor Mum. It must have been hell. She'd been the prettiest and brightest girl in her village. Lord knows what made her choose Dad. Perhaps she thought she liked the strong silent type and by the time she found she didn't I was on the way and she was trapped and they had to get married.

She told me all about it once when she was in a rage about something or other. I certainly had no hang-ups about starting off this life the wrong side of the blanket but I'd resolved never to be trapped in the same way. No thanks. Not yours truly.

After a week Rachel was on the mend and allowed to rejoin the others. I was glad to get back to the usual routine and specially glad to see Marion again.

'I've got a message from Dan,' she said during our coffee break. 'He'll pick you up at six tomorrow.'

'Okay.'

She eyed me steadily over the rim of her mug. 'Don't get too involved with him, will you?'

'Please don't be jealous, Marion,' I said gently. 'There's no need. You are my friend. It's different with him.'

She nodded. 'I know. I admit I was a bit narked at first but I soon realized it was stupid. The trouble is Dan's done this sort of thing to friends of mine before and I don't want you to get hurt.'

'I won't. I promise.'

'Okay, but he can be a real devil, so don't stand any nonsense.'

'Right.' I breathed easily again, glad *that* conversation was over.

A few minutes later the postman arrived and Jane handed me a letter. It was from Dad. He hardly ever put pen to paper so I wondered what was up. I tore open the envelope and a newspaper cutting fell out. Pinned to it was brief note.

'Dear Nell, thought this might interest you. Hope all goes well. Had to take the cat to the vet last week. Fur balls in the gut as usual. All the best. Love. Dad.'

The cutting was from our local paper and when I opened it out I found myself looking at a photograph of a smiling Mark, arm-in-arm with a dazzling blonde in full wedding gear. Underneath the caption read 'Mr and Mrs Mark Field on the steps of St Mary's Church, Leeds, after their wedding on 18th July.' And it burbled on about how popular Mark had been and how everyone wished him and Jackie great happiness in their new home.

Of course I'd known that I'd hear about it sooner or later but I was totally unprepared for my own reaction. As I stared, the photograph began to swim before my eyes and I felt as though something was choking me. Stumbling blindly from the room I ran out to the garden and headed straight for the lake, where I threw myself down in the long grass and cried my eyes out.

After no more tears would come I just lay there, racked by the occasional shivery spasm but vaguely comforted by the warm sun-soaked earth. Gradually I became aware of tiny insects scurrying to and fro and up and down the grass in front of my eyes and I thought how giant-like I must seem to them and wondered how many fragile homes I was crushing with my huge body.

Life isn't fair, I thought, be you girl or spider.

Suddenly I heard someone charging along the path whistling loudly and before I had time to move, Jim Blair, carrying a pair of oars over his shoulder, tripped over me.

'Lord, you gave me a fright,' he said.

Sitting up, I tried out a watery smile. 'Sorry.'

'Hey,' he unloaded the oars on the grass and crouched down. 'What's the matter? You look like a wet Sunday in Wapping.'

'Nothing,' I sniffed. 'I'm getting a cold, that's all.'

He nodded sympathetically. 'Rotten for you. Would a row on the lake make you feel better?'

I gave a weak laugh. 'Kill or cure? Okay. Why not?'

Getting up I stuffed the cutting in my pocket, brushed the grass from my skirt and followed him along the path.

Just around the corner we came upon an old rowing boat tied to a post on a makeshift landing-stage. I'd come across it before on my travels round the park and wondered who used it.

'Get in, then,' Jim said.

I jumped aboard and the whole thing rocked and rolled like crazy.

'Watch it or you'll have her over,' Jim warned, handing me the oars. 'Can you row?'

'Of course,' I said, settling the heavy things in the metal jobs each side of the boat.

'Okay.' Untying the rope, he threw it into the boat. 'Off you go then.' And turning away he walked off whistling.

I stared disbelievingly at his retreating back. 'Hey,' I called. 'Aren't you coming too?'

He turned around. 'I thought you might want to be alone.'

Nervously I watched the gap slowly widening between me and the landing-stage. 'No. That is, er . . . my rowing's not all that hot.'

'Well, can you swim?'

'Yes but . . .'

'Because if you can't you'd better sit down and stop rocking the boat.'

I sat. By now the gap had widened considerably. I gulped. Better come clean. 'Matter of fact I've never been in a boat before, so I don't know what to do.'

'Well that's different,' he said, walking back to the lake. 'I thought you said you could row. I must have misheard you. Now . . .' he fingered his chin thoughtfully. 'How am I going to get you back?'

I seized the rope and threw it at him. 'With this, of course.'

He caught it and stood there nodding like a village idiot. 'Oh, yeah. I was forgetting.'

He was teasing me, of course, but I pretended not to notice.

After he'd hauled in the boat he got in and plomped himself down on the back seat facing me.

'But aren't you going to row?' I asked.

'No, you are,' he said, neatly coiling the rope on the floor. 'And this, by the way, is called the painter.'

'Oh yeah?'

'And those things the oars are in are the rowlocks and I'm sitting in the stern and the sharp end is called the bow.'

'Amazing,' I said dryly. I mean I was pretty annoyed. I'd naturally assumed he would row but there he was lolling in the stern while I struggled clumsily with the wretched oars. Moving that old boat was like trying to shift a two-decker bus without wheels. I kept snagging water weeds and lily-pads or missing the water altogether and practically falling backwards off the seat. But I knew Jim – who just sat there grinning – was waiting for me to give up so I gritted my teeth and battled on. After all, I reasoned, anyone could row. It was just . . . (I could feel my face getting red from sheer frustration) just a matter of . . . getting . . . the knack . . .

By now I'd managed to propel us into a mass of water lilies and, push and pull as I might, I couldn't get us out again.

'Ship your oars,' Jim said. It was the first time he'd opened his mouth since we became, so to speak, lily-locked.

'What do you mean?'

'Pull them back into the rowlocks.'

'Why?'

'Because they might slip into the water,' he explained patiently. 'Then you'd have to swim after them. I take it you *can* swim?'

'I said I could.'

'So you did. Well I hope for your sake your swimming's better than your rowing.' He peered over the side of the boat. 'Do you want to have another go at getting us out of this?'

'No. You do it.'

We changed places and he rowed us clear with a couple of strong strokes and sent us whisking along in the smooth water.

'You didn't do too badly for a landlubber,' he said.

'Huh!' I scoffed flicking water at him. He looked nice when he smiled. He was so dark that it was hard to believe he was English. With his black eyes and hair and his tanned face and neck he could easily have been Italian, or French maybe. As we glided along, chatting idly about this and that, a lovely feeling of safety came over me. It had nothing to do with Jim's expert boat handling, it was something about him, himself. A deep sense of peace, tranquillity, confidence — I don't know exactly. I only know that I had a growing urge to tell him about Mark's marriage.

'I had a bit of a shock today,' I said trailing my fingers in the cool water.

He didn't reply immediately then he said, 'Want to talk about it?'

Did I? Now it came to it I wasn't all that sure. While I was deciding an amazing thing happened. It was as though part of me was suddenly on the bank looking at us in the boat in the middle of the lake. I distinctly saw my fair, curly hair and my yellow T-shirt and Jim, relaxed over the oars, his brown arms resting across his legs. All around us the water, broken by patches of white, pink and red lilies, shone bright as a mirror. The bushes on the island in the centre of the lake cast short black shadows on the gleaming surface and the trees on the far bank towered darkly, their leaves densely massed against the blue sky. Everything was still. Even the coots and moorhens, usually so active, seemed caught in a frozen moment of time.

Then it was gone and I was inside myself again, in the boat, staring at Jim who was staring at me.

Chapter 9

'Are you okay?' he asked.
  'Yes. But just now I . . .'
  'What?'

'Oh nothing.' I didn't want him to think I was raving. Putting my hand in my pocket I fingered the newspaper cutting, then I took it out and looked at it. 'Someone I'm very fond of has just got himself married.'

He took the cutting, looked at it briefly then handed it back.

'Your boyfriend?'

'No. He was the social worker assigned to me when I had a sort of breakdown.'

Jim didn't fall apart with shock, he just nodded slowly and said, 'Those people can become very important. You get to depend on them.'

'That's right,' I agreed eagerly. 'You see after Mum went . . . there was no one else around and I felt so awful. Mark was kind and I . . .' I stopped as though clogged up in some vital part.

After a bit he said gently, 'It was awful when my mum died, too, so I know how you feel.'

There it was – the perfect let-out. I wouldn't have to say any more but I suddenly felt a compelling need to tell the truth for once.

'She didn't die,' I said quickly. 'One day when I got back from school she'd gone. Vanished. After a couple of days Dad told the police, who said they'd make enquiries. But they warned us they couldn't do much because married people left home every day and had a right to do so. They said not to worry as she'd probably be back when she got fed up – like most of them.'

'Go on.'

'That's it, really. She never phoned or wrote or anything.'

'So where is she now?'

'Dunno. Dead for all I know.'

He was silent for a moment, staring into the distance, then he said, 'Poor her. She must have been very unhappy.'

'Huh!' I snorted. 'She must? What about us? My dad lost a stone in weight and I nearly lost my marbles.'

'Yes, poor you, too. Of course.' He shook his head, lost for words. I sensed his distress and I felt vaguely comforted.

'I've never talked about it,' I said. 'Except to the doctor – and Mark.'

'The social worker?'

'Yes.'

'Let's have another look at him.'

I gave him the cutting and he studied it carefully, as if he was trying to see through the photograph to the actual people. 'He's got good taste in women,' he announced finally. 'And he looks as if he knows where h's going.'

'He's not pushy or anything,' I said, bridling at the implied criticism.

He handed back the cutting. 'There's nothing wrong with ambition. It's the lengths people go to in order to achieve their ambitions that frighten me.'

'Aren't you ambitious, then?'

'Sure.'

'What for?'

'The usual things, I suppose. Money, security, happiness. You see I'd like us – Dad and me – to expand our business; offer a wider range of services, but Dad's not too keen. I want to apply for a government-sponsored business course but he won't hear of it. Oh well . . .' He gave a resigned shrug. 'There's a whole lot more to life than being a commercial success.'

'Really? What?' I was probably the only person at

Finchings who had ever held a proper conversation with Jim. I couldn't let him stop now.

He grinned sheepishly. 'I don't want to bore you.'

'If you bore me I'll dive off the boat,' I promised rashly.

'Well, I think too many people are so busy trying to "get on" that they forget how to live. Come the end of a day, a month, a year and all they have to look back on are meetings, confrontations, journeys from one place to another. Not much else. A few pints in the pub. A laugh with the boys. I don't want it to be like that.'

I had an unwelcome picture of Dad bustling around the ironmongery at Mr Pierce's beck and call all day and dozing in front of the telly all evening. Not like that either!

'How would you like it to be, then?' I asked.

Jim tugged thoughtfully at his left ear. 'It's difficult, perhaps impossible, to put into words but you know how sometimes, without warning, you are acutely aware of everything going on around you? More than usual, I mean. Everything seems sharp, clear as crystal . . .'

'Yes! Yes!' I was on the edge of my seat. So it happened to him too . . .

'You see and hear all the normal things, doors banging, people talking – all that – but you are intensely aware of another dimension, one you can't see or hear but which is there just the same. Oh dear, I'm not making much sense, am I?'

'Go on.'

'It's as though, for a few seconds, everything is clear and you are, in every sense, alive. Alive to the whole of creation I mean. It doesn't happen very often but when

66

it does you really feel you've been allowed to glimpse the secret of life itself.'

As he spoke his face looked transformed and radiant like that of an Old Testament mystic.

'Go on,' I breathed.

'That's about it.' His expression returned to normal. 'My real ambition is to live, fully live every minute and not waste a second in the semi-conscious state so many people stumble around in.'

'That's boredom. Everyone is bored some time or other,' I argued gently. 'Even you, I bet.'

'Sure. Often. Although I believe boredom simply means you can't dredge up enough interest in things going on around you. But negative emotions are inescapable and must be accepted. Anyway, nothing stays the same so there's generally a limit to how long boredom or anger or misery lasts, thank God!'

'When Mum went off I was relieved for a couple of days,' I admitted. 'Then I was worried, then angry, then I got ill. I couldn't go to school, or anywhere else for that matter, because I kept getting giddy and sick. And I couldn't stop crying. That's when they finally decided that they'd better do something and they sent Mark along . . .' I leant over the side of the boat to hide the tears in my eyes and Jim started rowing again. The steady motion of the boat as we circled the lake and the sound of the blades dipping through the water were soothing. Soon my mind went into a kind of trance, when Mum and Mark and all the other things that worried me ceased to exist, and I was only aware of the sun on my back and the cool water running between my fingers and Jim's strong, brown arms as he pulled on the oars and relaxed, pulled and relaxed . . .

It all felt so right and easy that we might have known each other for a thousand years.

Hours (or minutes) later a cloud passed over the sun.

'Better go in now,' Jim said pulling for the bank. 'I've got an appointment with a combine harvester this afternoon.'

Suddenly I remembered something important. 'By the way, Jim,' I said casually, 'about the other night . . .'

He looked blank. 'What do you mean?'

I shifted uncomfortably. 'You know . . . when you were walking up the drive . . .'

His brow cleared. 'Oh you mean the evening I went down to see old Harry who lives in the Lodge. What about it?' Jumping on to the landing-stage he secured the boat to the mooring post.

'Well,' I said jumping after him. 'You probably saw me and a . . . a friend.'

'Oh it was you was it? Yes, I saw Dan Glease larking in the bushes with some girl or other. I didn't know it was you.'

It was embarrassing but I had to press on. 'So you know Dan, do you?'

He reached into the boat for the oars. 'Sure. We were at school together. Can't say we were exactly mates, though. In fact . . .' Shouldering the oars he walked on to the path. 'I'd be a bit careful with him if I were you.'

'Oh? In what way?'

He looked back over his free shoulder. 'You know what way, Nell, don't be daft. You're not that green.'

'Thanks for the advice,' I said, thoroughly nettled by his tone. Why did everyone want to spike my relationship with Dan?

He nodded briefly and strode away whistling again.

I set off in the opposite direction. To tell the truth, having unburdened my soul, I was now slightly worried. Telling people things about yourself is like handing them a loaded gun which they can fire at your head any time they wish. On the other hand you've got to trust someone some time in your life. Well haven't you?

Chapter 10

It was lunchtime when I arrived back at the house. Although I'd skipped a couple of hours' duty no one asked me where I'd been. Marion cast a few sympathetic looks in my direction but she kept quiet, too.

We spent the afternoon on the beach with the kids, and believe me it needed all of us to ensure everyone had a good time and no one drowned. Roy Somers, for example, crawled into the sea and would have kept crawling until he was under if I hadn't stopped him, whereas Janice Toms yelled blue murder every time anyone tried to get her to paddle. Marion and I built a million sand castles, filled umpteen buckets with water, threw stones at tin cans and blew up water wings until we both felt we could do with a nice holiday in central Manchester.

After all the fun we piled into the bus and drove home, tired but happy. Putting the kids to bed was a breeze because they all went out like a light as soon as their heads touched the pillow.

Supper was the best time of day at Finchings. The dining room faced west and the evenings were so warm that the windows were always open. You almost felt you were eating in the garden. It was lovely watching the shadows lengthen and the sun sink lower and lower until zonk, it had gone and you were conscious of the half-light and the pungent scent of flowers drifting in on the night air.

All the other helpers lived out, so there were only Bill and Jane and me for supper. Gradually we got into a routine: Bill cooked the meal while I laid the table and Jane did her accounts. Then I cleared the plates while Bill served the next course. When we finished eating it was my job to stack the huge dishwasher and leave the kitchen tidy.

I continued to prefer Jane to Bill, perhaps because she took more trouble to get to know me. Bill had very strong opinions about things and people and I was a little afraid of stepping out of line. Neither of them asked me probing personal questions, although they often wanted to know what I thought about life in general, so I was utterly disconcerted when Jane suddenly said,

'You must think Bill and I a pretty heartless pair not to have mentioned your mother.'

'M-Mum?' I said apprehensively.

'Yes. The car accident must have been a terrible shock for you and your father. We were horrified when Marion told us about it. I don't know why exactly but we'd both assumed you had a full complement of parents. I wish Peggy Lawton had warned us.'

'I asked her not to,' I said quickly.

Bill looked across at Jane. 'There you are. I told you she wouldn't want to talk about it.'

'No, we won't talk about it,' Jane said. 'But at least we can tell Nell that we understand how she's feeling.'

I knew she was thinking about my two-hour absentee period in the morning.

'Well, don't get maudlin, my love,' Bill pleaded, obviously embarrassed by the turn of the conversation. 'More salad, Nell?'

I helped myself, grateful to him for changing the subject. Obviously Jane had asked Marion what was the matter with me when I dashed from the room during the coffee break and Marion had said it was something to do with my letter, possibly connected with my mother's death in a car accident. Now it would be common knowledge and I'd have to stick with the story. It made me thoroughly nervous and after that evening I found myself being extra careful about what I said. If the least exaggeration crept to the edge of my tongue I squashed it like I squashed the odd wasp zooming hopefully around the kitchen. I figured the only person who could blow my story was Jim Blair. Why oh why hadn't I kept my trap shut? I'd never been one for blabbing my troubles around like some of the kids at school, so what on earth had made me confess all to Jim? The best thing I could do was keep well out of his way and hope he would forget all about it.

Our paths often crossed, of course. Either he came into the kitchen while I was helping to prepare a meal, or we met in the garden when I was playing with the kids. If we did bump into each other I said, 'Hi Jim,' with a bright smile and hurried on. He never tried to delay me and soon I almost persuaded myself that the morning on the lake had never happened.

Almost. Sometimes when I saw him crossing the

park I had a mad impulse to dash after him and somehow recapture that strange understanding we'd experienced so briefly, but I guessed he'd now have heard the tale about Mum's fatal accident and he must have concluded that I was either mad or a pathological liar.

Fortunately, I didn't have much time to dwell on it because Dan began to turn up most evenings on his motor bike. I could see how much Bill disapproved of him, so to avoid embarrassment we always went out. I'd have been quite happy to spend some evenings with his family but Dan always wanted to meet up with his cronies at the amusement arcade, where the boys spent hours playing the machines and we girls stood around pretending not to be bored. To tell the truth I didn't have anything in common with any of them. The boys regarded me as Dan's property and left me strictly alone and the girls made it clear they thought I was barmy to work my guts out in a place like Finchings when I could be taking it easy and collecting my unemployment along with them. To be fair, most of them had tried to get a job but none of them had a CSE to their name so they faced stiff competition for the few jobs that were going.

After leaving the arcade we generally drifted along to one of the sea-front cafés for coffee and that. We were supposed to take it in turns paying but my turn seemed to come round more often than the others.

'You're the only one working so you can afford it,' Dan would say cheerfully. Then he would murmur in my ear, 'I'll make it up to you later, doll,' which always meant stopping in a field on the way home for lots of french kissing and groping on his side and desperate defence tactics on mine.

Although it was an energetic half-hour it was the part of the evening I enjoyed best. I was really gone on Dan, and his kissing transported me to somewhere else. In fact if I hadn't been so plumb scared I might have let him go too far. But I didn't and he seemed quite happy about it all, so naturally I assumed things were fine between us. But that was before the midnight picnic.

We moved off at 10 p.m., Marion and I and Dan and the gang. It was a bright moonshiny night and as we roared away in convoy I couldn't help thinking how exciting life was compared to a year ago.

We had previously chosen a rocky cove outside the town where we were unlikely to be apprehended by an enthusiastic copper for breaching the public peace; after parking the bikes we carried the picnic stuff, rugs, cassettes, etc., acrossa sloping field to the edge of the cliff. Then someone discovered the coastal path and we set off, slipping and sliding on the crumbling chalk to the accompaniment of groans and curses from the boys and squeaks and giggles from the girls.

When we reached the bottom we spread out the rugs, got a Michael Jackson tape going, lit up our fags (well, not me, of course) and sat around telling stupid jokes and falling about like idiots. Quite honestly I think everyone felt a bit awkward. Without their bikes or the pinball machines the boys were like fish out of water and their general sense of unease seemed reflected in the girls' shrieks and cackles. Although most of them had lived near the coast all their lives it seemed as though they'd never been so conscious of the powerful, mysterious water rippling inkily away into the darkness. I think it scared them because in spite of the hot sultry night not one of them would venture into the sea. I could hardly believe it.

'Coming in?' I asked Dan.

'You must be joking,' he said, puffing away at his fag.

So I nipped behind a rock, stripped to my bikini and running down to the water I slipped into its silky shallows. It was fantastic. Still warm, it swirled smoothly around my limbs as I swam on and on following the silvery ribbon of light towards its source, the moon. Then I lay on my back and gazed up at the stars, my mind humming like an electric wire and my body borne along like a piece of floating debris. Perhaps I would end up on a South Sea Island . . .

Suddenly there was a lot of splashing and a voice called. 'Nell?'

Dan! So he'd decided to come in after all. I trod water while he swam alongside.

'What the hell do you think you're up to?' he asked rudely.

'What do you mean?'

'We've all been yelling our heads off. Didn't you hear us?'

'No. What's the matter?'

'We thought you'd drowned, that's all. Marion's got her knickers in a real twist.'

'I'm sorry,' I said contritely. 'I didn't think.'

'Dan?' a voice called from the shore. 'Is everything okay?'

Dan cupped his hand to his mouth. 'Yeah. Everything's fine.'

'I'm really sorry,' I said again.

He seemed slightly mollified by my apology. 'Oh

74

well. Of course I knew you'd be okay so I wasn't worried.' He swam off a little way. 'Come on, let's swim round into the next cove and see what it's like.'

In retrospect I can see that it was stupid of me to agree. It was bound to lead to trouble, Dan and me half naked on a beach in the moonlight. Especially as, by now, the rest of the party would have divided into pairs and be merrily snogging away. So when we emerged from the water and he immediately launched into a heavy session I wasn't particularly alarmed. But after a while it all became too much and as he wasn't about to take no for an answer I shoved him off and dashed back into the shallow water.

Getting to his feet he began to throw tiny stones at me. His aim was true and they stung like pin-pricks. I could tell he was angry.

'I don't understand you,' he complained as I ducked under the water to escape being hit. 'One minute you're as hot as a roast chestnut and the next you're fighting me off like a wildcat. What's wrong?'

'Nothing,' I said. 'So get off my back.'

He stopped throwing stones. 'We've got to get this straight.'

'Get what straight?'

'Come off it. You know what. Look, we can't talk with you out there and me here.'

'I want to go back to the others. I'm getting cold.'

'I'll warm you up.'

'Yeah.'

'No, seriously. I've got something to tell you. I think you'll be pleased.'

'Do let's go, Dan.'

'After I've told you.'

I gave in. 'Okay. But don't try anything on.' I walked back up the beach and we sat down on the stones facing each other.

'You're always at me to get a job . . .' he began.

'No I'm not.'

'Well, I know you don't think I try hard enough.'

I laughed. 'Since when do you care what I think?'

'That's where you're wrong. I do care, so, to cut a long story short, I think I've got one.'

'I don't believe it! What is it?'

'Trainee barman at the Feathers.'

'That's really great. Isn't your mum thrilled?'

'I haven't told her. I haven't told anyone but you because it's not definite yet.'

'When will you know?'

'In a few days. So what do you think of Danny boy now? Deserve a cuddle do I?' Catching my hand, he pulled me towards him.

'Dan, wait . . .'

'I've only done it for you,' he breathed against my lips.

'Please wait . . .'

He groaned. 'No, I've waited too long.'

'Listen!' Grabbing his hands I held them in a vice. 'Do you realize that we never talk? I mean talk about anything important. You're always fooling around with that bunch over there. The only time we are ever alone is on the back of the bike or rolling around a cornfield on the way back to Finchings. We are still strangers. I don't know anything about you and you don't know me.'

He shook his hands free. 'What is there to talk about? I'm here. You're here. That's enough isn't it?'

I sighed. How could I make him understand? I was

fed up with the amusement arcade and the bowling alley and tearing mindlessly around with the gang.

'No it's not enough,' I said. 'Don't you see?'

'No.'

I gave up. He'd never understand. 'Anyway,' I said, 'I'm not ready for anything serious. After all, I'm only sixteen.'

'Who said anything about being serious?'

'But if you and I . . . Wouldn't it be serious then?'

He laughed. 'Where have you been hiding? Look around. Are Bob and Sandra serious? Or Jeff and Rose? She's only fifteen.'

'You mean they are all . . .?'

'Of course they are, dumbo! It's no big deal, you know. People do it all the time.'

Yeah, people like my mum, who found herself pregnant and in a situation beyond her control.

'I need to think about it a bit more,' I said.

Dan got to his feet. 'Your trouble is you think too much. Anyway, since there's no point in staying here we'd better get back to the others.' Diving into the water he headed for the other cove.

For a full minute I stayed sitting on the beach watching him bob away, his arms flashing white in the moonlight. I don't think I've ever felt so alone, not even after Mum left. It was no good telling myself that he didn't matter, because he did. Being with him was like warming myself in front of a cheerful blaze. I enjoyed it and I enjoyed the element of danger in our relationship, the feeling that if I got too close to the heat I might catch fire myself. But it was obvious from our conversation and his impatient attitude that we couldn't go on like this. ' — or get off the pot' was one of my Dad's ruder expressions. Now I could see what he meant. It was up to me and just at the moment I couldn't see what to do.

Back in the other cove Jeff had lit a fire and was cooking a batch of bangers. The strains of Frankie Goes To Hollywood wafted across the beach and everyone seemed to be having a good time. Marion and her date were the only ones not indulging in heavy necking, so after dressing I sat with her while Dan took over the frying pan from Jeff.

'Having fun?' I asked Marion.

She jerked her head towards her date Pete, lying prone on the stones nearby. 'Yeah. I'm having a ball.' She half grinned and I was surprised to see her eyes swimming with tears.

'What's the matter with me, Nell?' she whispered.

I squeezed her hand sympathetically. 'Nothing. You've latched on to a zombie, that's all.'

'Then they are all zombies. I mean everyone I go out with.'

Poor Marion. She always had this trouble with her love life. Usually she joked about it – B.O., bad breath and so on – but underneath it hurt like hell. For some reason the boys just didn't fancy her. Of course she was taller than most of them and she dressed badly, but I had the feeling that if she were more self-confident the rest wouldn't matter so much. The only time she was really sure of herself was with the kids at Finchings and I was certain that if only she could carry that sense of her own worth into her social life things would soon be different for her.

'Maybe we could do something about your hair soon,' I suggested. 'And maybe we could buy you some new gear. I mean – don't take this wrong – sometimes you look as if you're wearing your Mum's cast-offs.'

She made a wry face. 'I probably am. I've never been any good with clothes but that isn't the only problem. It's money. I've only managed to save twenty pounds.'

'That's okay. I've got a bit saved too so I'll lend you some and you can pay me back when you're flush.'

'Nell, you wouldn't!'

'Course I will.'

'But I couldn't possibly take it.'

'Then I'll have to stuff it down your throat, won't I?'

A loud snore from Pete suddenly punctuated the silence.

'The hills are alive with the sound of music,' Marion said and we both burst out laughing.

Chapter 11

The next few days were taken up with the departure of our kids to their various homes after their holiday. I was sad to see them go, knowing that most of them would return to mothers who had too many problems of their own to give the kids all the attention they really needed. As Rachel's mother was still in hospital Jane agreed to keep her as long as necessary, which was great as we'd all grown so fond of her.

Within a week the new batch of kids were settling down well. Jane insisted on all the staff spending time each day getting to know the children personally and during the coffee and tea breaks we would compare our findings. Now and again one of us would discover something about a particular child that none of the others had noticed, which made the whole exercise worthwhile. Jane was good at making everyone feel they were contributing something valuable to the life at Finchings.

Much of the work, however, was routine, and as bed-making and spud-peeling doesn't exactly strain the brain I had plenty of time to think about my Big Problem. It was obvious that if I didn't go along with Dan's idea of a 'good' relationship I couldn't hope to keep him much longer; on the other hand if I did go along with it he might take what was on offer and go in search of fresher fields. Quite a dilemma. Briefly I considered what, in the light of her own experience, Mum would have advised. But then I realized she'd probably have thrown the book at me and called me a disgusting little tramp or something – which, of course, was the reason I'd never have asked her in the first place.

Soon after the new kids arrived Marion and I took the afternoon off together and went shopping. With the twenty quid she'd saved and the twenty I planned to lend her we thought we'd be able to kit her out brilliantly. That was before we started looking at prices. In the end we settled for a pair of red flatties (her shoes looked like clapped-out Chinese junks) a mauve sun dress with red stitching around the hem, a pair of black pedal-pushers, a jazzy shirt and a red cotton jacket we found at the bottom of a heap in a second-hand shop.

When we got home she tried on all the gear in her bedroom. As I watched her I could see both our reflections in the mirror and I couldn't help wondering why I looked okay in a sail-cloth skirt and navy top while

Marion, in almost the same get-up, managed to look frumpy. Admittedly she was all arms and legs and bushy hair but it wasn't only that. It had something to do with the air of dejection she carried about permanently. Hardly surprising when you came to think of it as life had treated Marion far worse than it had treated me. To start with her dad hadn't just disappeared, he'd upped and died. As if that wasn't bad enough Nick had then blighted an exciting career and nearly killed himself and Dan – who should have supported his mum in her hour of need – had continued to mooch around with his mates, borrowing cash from all and sundry. (Being attracted to him didn't blind me to his faults!) It had been left to Marion to prop up her stricken family, both emotionally and financially. No wonder it had all got her down.

What she needed, I decided, was to change her image, see herself differently. It wouldn't cure her problems but it might cheer her up and start other people, notably boys, seeing her in a different light. They might even be intrigued by the 'new' Marion.

Right now she was rather pleased with herself. 'Do you think I look like a model?' she laughed, twirling around to display the black cut-offs and multicoloured shirt.

'Well, straighten up and show the world you've got some boobs,' I said.

She giggled. 'But I haven't.'

'Try.'

'Like that?' She thrust out the pathetic specimens.

'Yeah, that's better. A couple of gnat bites are better than nothing. See?' I pushed out my own until they strained against my T-shirt.

'Mine are bigger than yours,' she said.

'Bet they're not.'

'Bet they are!'

We strutted around the room making our boobs as big as possible then we collapsed laughing.

When we sobered up Marion peered at herself in the mirror. 'The gear's okay but what am I going to do about the rest of me?'

I looked her over critically. 'Your face is basically okay. Your eyebrows need a bit of careful plucking and you'd look better without all that blusher and stuff. Your hair is the trouble. It's so wild and woolly in the wrong sort of way. It really needs cutting and styling.'

Marion shook her head gloomily. 'No dice. After today I'm skint. Cleaned out. Hey!' She swung around to face me, her eyes alight. 'Couldn't you cut it?'

'Me?' I squeaked. 'But I don't know how. I've only ever cut Dad's hair and that's dead easy because he hasn't got much.'

'Oh do have a go, Nell.'

'What if you hate the result?'

'Then it will be my fault for asking you.'

'I dunno . . .'

'Be a pal.'

'Oh all right.' She sat down and I draped a towel around her shoulders and reluctantly took the proffered scissors.

'This will probably be the end of a beautiful friendship,' I said, grasping a piece of hair. 'Anyway, here goes.'

It was like cutting through wire wool. Frowning with concentration I clipped the hair into a close fringe. Then I just lopped it off all over her head. The stuff dropped around my feet like sacrifical locks. It felt as though I was preparing her to take her final vows in a convent or something. Every time I hesitated she said, 'Go on. Take off a bit more.'

As I shaped one side I noticed something very interesting was happening. The more of her face I uncovered the more her pretty, heartshaped jawline and wide cheekbones came into view. The longer I continued the more excited I became and by the time the job was completed I felt as Michelangelo must have felt when he'd finished sculpting David. Marion, with a mere two inches of hair all over her head, was a real beauty.

'I can't believe it,' she said, turning her head this way and that on the longest neck I've ever seen. 'You're a real magician, Nell.'

I was pretty thunder-struck myself. 'I couldn't have done it if you'd had straight hair,' I admitted. 'The fact that it's got a will of its own made it impossible to go wrong.'

'Even so you're brilliant.'

'Oh well,' I smirked modestly. 'I have my moments.'

It was while we were clearing up the mess that she suddenly said, 'Things aren't right with you and Dan, are they?'

You could have knocked me over with the proverbial feather! 'What makes you think that?' I asked.

Marion shrugged. 'I just know you both so well. And I bet I even know what the trouble is.'

I didn't say anything but I flushed bright pink. Of course Marion saw it at once.

'I just don't want you to get hurt,' she said. 'Have you ever done it?'

'Done what?' As if I didn't know what she meant!

'It . . . you know.'

'No.' I paused in the middle of stuffing a bushel of hair into the waste basket and sat back on my heels. After all I'd been wanting to talk to someone, so why not Marion? 'Have you?' I asked.

She grinned wickedly. 'Chance would be a fine thing!'

But I couldn't bring myself to smile. Instead I blurted out, 'Marion, I'm so worried. I've got a feeling he'll dump me soon if I don't do what he wants.'

I desperately needed her to say something encouraging, perhaps even tell me to go ahead, but she didn't. She just sat staring at herself in the mirror as if she still couldn't believe what she saw. I wondered if she'd even heard me.

Suddenly she swung round on the stool. 'Well, you'd be a right nana if you let yourself be blackmailed into it.'

'But what if – deep down – I want to?'

'Do you?'

'Part of me does.'

She made a funny face. 'That's the part we're always being warned against. What about the other part?'

'That's the part that doesn't know.'

'Hm. Would you be very miserable if he dumped you?'

I nodded wordlessly. It hurt to think about it, let alone speak about it.

She could see I was distressed so she didn't say anything. I mean, what could she say? We just sat there staring into space. I was thinking that no one else can really advise you on something as fundamental as sex. You just have to make up your own mind.

Finally Marion stood up. 'Well, just be sure you don't plunge into something you'll regret afterwards, that's all. Now let's go down and amaze the family with the new me. Nick's a bit gloomy these days — a good belly laugh is just what he needs.'

Chapter 12

In the days following Marion's amazing transformation my fears about Dan grew. The sound of his bike roaring up the drive was noticeable only by its absence, and I spent the evenings yawning in front of the telly or watching swallows skim the surface of the swimming pool for insects.

'Not going out tonight?' Bill would ask innocently.

'Nope,' I'd say casually, but the I-told-you-so look in his eyes made me want to throw his boeuf à la this or that straight back in his smug face.

It was lonely. You see, I'd been going out with Dan for quite a while and although the amusement arcade had its limitations, an evening there had to be better than one spent rattling around on my tod at Finchings.

To be honest, I couldn't really believe that he'd finally chucked me — he'd acted too keen the last time we'd met. Deep down I suspected that he was giving me a taste of what it would be like if he actually decided to stop seeing me. Not nice, I can tell you — it was the most restless, miserable week of my stay.

One evening I was lying on the sun-warmed stones by the pool reading yet another thriller when Jim Blair appeared. He gave me a cheerful wave, stripped off to his swimming trunks and dived in. As I watched him ploughing to and fro, his arms slicing powerfully through the water, I thought how purposeful he was about everything he did. If Jim swam then he swam — no messing. If he rowed, he rowed. If he played with the kids he entered into the game with gusto as if he was one of them. I liked that.

After twenty minutes he climbed out, shook off the water (like Plod when he'd been into the sea) then sat down next to me.

'What are you reading?'

'Dick Francis.' I showed him the cover.

'Do you read much?'

'Only when I've nothing better to do.'

'So you're bored. Where's lover boy?'

'I don't know what you mean,' I said coldly.

'Our local Lothario, Dan Glease.'

I'd no idea who Lothario was but I could see he didn't mean it as a compliment. 'I expect he's started his new job,' I said. 'It means he'll be working evenings.'

'Dan working?' Jim raised a pair of incredulous eyebrows. 'What's he doing, then?'

'Barman at the Feathers.'

He shook his head. 'Not a chance. Archie Stobbs started at the Feathers last week. I know because he's a mate of mine.'

'But Dan said . . .' I frowned. What exactly had he said? Something about them letting him know. 'Well, perhaps he didn't get it after all,' I finished lamely.

Jim stretched out on the stones. 'Archie's been in line for that job for weeks. Perhaps you got hold of the wrong end of the stick.'

But I knew I hadn't. Why had he gone to the trouble

of pretending he might get the job? To make me think he was really a solid guy at heart so that I would fall confidently into his arms or to raise his own self-esteem? Being without a job for so long must be pretty self-destroying, even for someone as pleased with himself as Dan. I knew from Marion that he had tried for several jobs when he left school but as they hadn't worked out he'd stopped going for interviews. He once told me that he'd like to work in London but he didn't say what kind of work. Suddenly I felt very sorry for him, which was odd because only seconds before I'd been feeling sorry for myself. Somehow Dan's lie about the job made him seem a bit pathetic.

Anyway I must have been silent for longer than usual because Jim snapped his fingers and said, 'A penny for them?'

I smiled and shook my head. 'Not worth it.'

He sat up and rubbed his hair with his towel, then he combed it with his fingers and vaguely attempted to push aside his fringe. It swung back immediately, like a shiny black curtain, and I had a strange urge to touch it to see if it was as silky as it looked. I didn't, though. Impetuous I may be; mad I ain't.

'They've got a fair at Braywell,' he said. 'Why don't we go tomorrow evening?'

'Tomorrow?' It was Saturday. Dan always took me out on Saturday.

'It would make a change from Dick Francis.'

I didn't go much on fairs but it would be something to do and I was sick of hanging around waiting for Dan.

'Okay.'

'Right.' Jim pulled on his trousers and slung his towel over one shoulder. 'I'll have the pick-up outside at seven. Mind you wear those sexy pink dungarees.'

I blushed. It always confused me when Jim said something like that because it meant he was more aware of me than I thought. After he'd gone I did a few lengths of the pool and wondered what he would be like on a date. To tell the truth I felt a little nervous at the prospect. He had that effect on me. Don't ask me why.

I teamed the pink dungarees with a buttercup shirt and long dangly earrings. Checking up in front of the mirror I reminded myself of one of those stripy ice-creams; then the phrase 'good enough to eat' popped into my mind and I felt quite pleased.

'You'll wow 'em at the fair,' Jim said when I came out of the house.

'You won't,' I retorted, staring pointedly at his dirty working clothes.

'Sorry. I haven't had time to change yet. We'll go home and you can talk to Dad while I clean up.'

Jim and Mr Blair lived in an estate cottage a hundred metres down the lane, near the back entrance to Finchings. It could have been pretty but wasn't. Frankly it looked uncared for. The windows and door needed a fresh coat of green paint and although the garden was neat there were no flowers to soften the closely cut grass and the gravel path in front of the house. A patch of veg flourished at the back and that's where we found Mr Blair, in his shirt sleeves, industriously hoeing round the runner beans.

'Dad, this is Nell,' Jim said. 'I told you about her.'

I swallowed hard. What had he told his dad? About Mum? About Mark?

Mr Blair removed his pipe from his mouth and

regarded me with a pair of reassuringly kind brown eyes. 'Of course. You're the lass who was so good with that sick kid – Rachel, wasn't it?'

I sighed with relief. 'Yes. Rachel. She's still with us because her mother's in hospital.'

He nodded. 'It's a great gift being good with kids like that. I couldn't do it, sorry as I am for them.'

'They're just like other people except that they've got special problems.'

He shook his head. 'Maybe. Even so . . .'

'Dad, will you look after Nell while I get off this muck?' Jim said.

'With pleasure.' Mr Blair propped his hoe against a tree and winked at me. 'Take as long as you like, Jim boy.'

We sat on a rickety garden seat under an apple tree and Mr Blair puffed contentedly away at his pipe. He was stout and short and had a shock of wavy grey hair and a reddish face. Altogether he was very English and I couldn't see a trace of Jim in him.

'You a city girl, Nell?' he asked after a while.

'No. I've always lived in the country.'

'That so? You look like a city girl – if you don't mind my saying so.'

'It's the clothes, I expect. The earrings and that.'

He nodded. 'I expect so. My wife liked clothes. I had to get rid of all her pretty things when she died. It still seems wrong not having a woman about the house.'

'Perhaps you should marry again,' I said cheekily.

'Any offers?'

I grinned. 'Try me in ten years.'

We both laughed.

Mr Blair knocked out his pipe ash on the arm of the seat and made a few juicy blowing noises through the stem. 'You've got a sense of humour anyway.'

'Sometimes,' I said wryly.

He shrugged. 'That applies to us all. When I come home on a cold winter night and have to light the fire and get my own tea my sense of humour isn't all that good, I can tell you.'

'I know what you mean,' I said. And I meant it.

'Jim's a help, though,' Mr Blair conceded. 'He's good company and he always does his share. In fact if he didn't have this bee in his bonnet about the business I'd have no complaints about him.' He sighed heavily.

'What bee?' I asked. Well, he'd raised the subject, hadn't he?

He stared up into the apple tree as if trying to dislodge the fruit with his gaze. 'He wants to expand, invest in more machinery, advertise – all that nonsense.'

'Is it nonsense?'

He switched his gaze sharply to my face. 'Of course it is, girl. We're all right as we are. Not rich, I grant you, but we have all we need and we're happy enough – given the circumstances. Why work all the hours God sends just to make more money?'

'Young people need a bit of a challenge, Mr Blair,' I said gently. 'You can't blame Jim for wanting more out of life than you do.'

'It's a gamble, you know – putting oneself in hock to the bank and all that. I've never owed anyone money and I don't want to start now. Anyway, it all sounds so complicated and I wouldn't know where to begin.'

'But if Jim takes that business course he's so keen on he'll finish knowing exactly what to do. So there wouldn't be any need for you to worry.'

'That's what he says. I'm afraid we've had a few hard words about it. In fact, I won't talk about it any more because it only leads to a row. Life's too short, you know.' He blew noisily through his pipe again, obviously distressed. 'I don't know why I'm telling you all this. I should be entertaining you with witty conversation.'

'I expect it's on your mind.'

He nodded. 'It's hard to hand over the reins to your son.'

'That's understandable but . . .' I paused, wanting to reassure him but not wanting to give away too much of what Jim had told me.

'Yes?' He turned towards me and I suddenly felt that what I was about to say was tremendously important and might affect everyone's life, even mine. 'I'm pretty sure that Jim knows where he's going,' I said slowly. 'He's a thinker. He doesn't leap into things too quickly. At least — of course I don't know him very well — that's the way I see him.'

It wasn't a very profound comment but it seemed to satisfy him. He nodded several times, as if turning over what I'd said in his mind, then he grunted, stuffed his pipe into his pocket and stood up.

'Perhaps I'd better have another chat with him. Now what do you say to a taste of gooseberry wine? I've had it put by for a year or two so I think it's about ready to drink.'

Gooseberry wine? Oh well, try anything once, say I.

'Dad took quite a shine to you,' Jim said when we were on our way.

'How do you know?'

'He said you had a good head on your shoulders. Anyway, he brought out the gooseberry wine, didn't he? That's a mark of honour.'

'He's worried about your future.'

Jim made a wry face. 'He told you that, did he? What did you say?'

'That you'd thought it all out and knew what you were doing.'

'Good on you.'

'He said he was going to talk to you again.'

'Really? Well that's a step forward anyway. He has refused to discuss the subject for weeks.'

'Could he manage on his own while you were doing the course?'

Jim gave me a surprised look. 'You certainly have the knack of hitting the nail on the head don't you? Yes, he could now but in a few years he'll be too old, so I've got to get on with it as soon as possible.'

'I've got a feeling he'll listen this time.'

He smiled warmly at me. 'You seem to have been a great help. Thanks.'

'That's okay,' I said casually but inside I felt a real glow of pleasure.

We heard music coming from the fairground as soon as we got out of the pick-up in Braywell car park.

'I don't like the Octopus and things like that,' I said as we wound through the side streets.

'Then leave them alone,' he said matter-of-factly. 'You're here to enjoy yourself, aren't you?'

'Yeah.' Memories of Blackpool crowded in – Mum screaming her head off on the roller-coaster; Dad standing around looking bored and resigned; me pottering around the boating pool feel vaguely ashamed. Why on earth had I agreed to come today? My body gave an involuntary shiver.

'Cold?' Jim asked taking my arm.

'No. I was just remembering something.'

'It can't have been very pleasant.'

'It wasn't, so let's forget it.'

The fairground stood on the edge of the beach and was a fraction the size of the Blackpool Amusement Park. Even so it had everything a self-respecting fair should have: stalls selling candy and beads and dolls and cuddly toys; a merry-go-round, boat-dodgems, a ghost train, a huge wheel that span round high in the air, a Hall of Mirrors and goodness knows what else. Being Saturday night it was packed with people, all queuing for the rides and jostling each other out of the way and laughing like maniacs. The intense heat drove us straight to the ice-cream kiosk.

'Is it always as crowded as this?' I asked, staggering outside with my raspberry ripple.

'In the holiday season it is.' Jim tapped my shoulder bag with his free hand. 'Mind that unless you want it nicked.'

'Can we go on the ghost train?' I asked.

'I thought you didn't like that sort of thing.'

'No, it's heights and speed I can't stand. Things like the roller-coaster and the big whel.'

Jim bought tickets and we climbed into one of the little cars. In a trice we were off, careening through dark passages under soft, clingy spider-webs, and swinging round sharp corners into wet rubbery fingers that seemed to clutch at our hair while a ghostly laugh ricocheted around the tunnel, following us eerily as we sped on. At one point the train slowed down and a dim red light shone on a man's body hanging from a leafless tree, at another we seemed to be under attack from a whooping posse of Red Indians. Then we plunged into a lake and water flew up on all sides. Even though you knew it was a game it was still quite frightening and I found myself clinging to Jim for protection. After a while he put his arm around my shoulders and I snuggled closer when something really scared me.

As we slowed down and emerged into the light Jim took away his arm and I sat up.

'Enjoy that?' he asked.

I nodded happily. 'It was really scary, wasn't it?'

He grinned. 'Yeah. Really scary.'

'Now you're laughing at me.'

'That's because you're so funny,' he said, and the way he said it made me feel it was a sort of compliment.

'Can we have a go at the duck-shooting now?' I asked, jumping out of the train.

Jim groaned. 'I can see you're just beginning to get into your stride!'

We each had six shots and Jim managed to knock out all six of the metal ducks whizzing along the counter. Needless to say I shot wide of the mark every time. For his superb markmanship Jim won a goldfish in a plastic bowl, which we asked the man in charge to keep for us until later. After that we found the dodgem cars and tore around bashing each other and everyone else.

It was fun. I hadn't realized how much fun a fair could be if you just did the things you enjoyed. When we'd had enough we bought a couple of cans of Coke and flopped down on the beach below the fairground.

It was still light but dusk was coming on, creeping up on us from the sea. Behind us the fairground lights blazed like some fiery planet but in front the blue-grey water rolled calmly away until it melted into the blue-grey sky. Here and there the lights of a fishing boat twinkled faintly.

'It's a funny thing,' I said eventually, 'I've always had a bit of a hang-up about fun-fairs but after tonight I'm going to feel all right about them.'

Jim reached out and placed a hand over mine resting on the pebbles. 'I'm glad you're having fun. You've been looking a bit down lately.'

'Yeah well . . . that's all over now,' I said.

I've never made a quicker or more unexpected decision in my life. In fact I spoke before the thought was fully formed but once the words were out I knew I'd never go back on them. I was through with Dan Glease. There was nothing wrong with him and, except for leaving me alone during the past week, he hadn't treated me rottenly or anything but I couldn't stand the hassle over sex any longer. Quite suddenly — this is the important bit — I didn't want him any more. I don't know why. Perhaps it had something to do with Jim but I wasn't ready to examine that thought yet.

'Let's have our fortunes told by Madame Rosa,' I said. 'I'll pay.'

'No you won't.'

'But I haven't paid for anything yet.'

'Whose idea was this outing?'

'Yours but . . .'

'But nothing. I don't take girls out very often and when I do I expect to pay. I know it's square and I expect Women's Lib would burn me at the stake but there it is. Okay?'

'Are you too proud to take my money, then?'

'No. When I can't afford it and you can I'll let you pay.'

So there were to be other dates! I glanced shyly at him. I wasn't nervous of him any longer but he seemed so much older and wiser than any other boy I knew. Not for the first time I wondered why he was bothering with me.

He reached forward and tickled my nose with a blade of grass.

'Let's go, then. If you want your fortune told we'd better join the queue.'

We soon found Madam Rosa's red and yellow Romany caravan and stood hand in hand, like a couple of kids, gazing apprehensively up at the beaded curtain covering the doorway.

'Off you go, then,' Jim said.

'You first.'

He raised a quizzical eyebrow. 'Chicken, are you?'

'No, but you're older than me.'

'But it's beauty before brains every time.'

I gave him a little push. 'Stop fooling and go.'

He sighed. ' "Into the valley of death rode . . ." '

'Go *on*, Jim.'

'Okay. Don't go away, will you?' He ran up the steps.

'Jim . . .' I don't know what made me call but when he looked around, his black eyes gleaming under his swingy hair, something inside me did a surprised flip, like a pancake being tossed in the pan. It was as if I recognized him from somewhere way back in my life – or in another life – and I had been waiting for him to turn up again. At the same time I desperately wanted to stop him from going inside the caravan in case – I know this sounds childish – he never came out again.

'Yes?' he said.

I swallowed, aware that I was being stupid, irrational. 'Oh nothing.'

He waited for a second then waved cheerfully and

disappeared, leaving me staring worriedly at the swaying beads.

I was still staring when I felt a hand grip my shoulder and, twisting round, I found myself face to face with Dan Glease.

Chapter 13

He was with the usual crowd, Bob and Mick and Jack and their girls plus others I didn't know. They all stood around munching popcorn and staring at me. You could have cut the atmosphere with a knife.

'We've been watching you,' Dan said. 'Having a good time, are you?'

'Yeah.'

Anthea giggled. 'With that wally?'

I ignored her. Anyway, she had terrible legs.

'We were in school together. Same class and that,' Dan went on. 'Did he tell you?'

'He told me.'

'I bet.' He winked at Mick. 'I wonder what else he told her.'

The goons cackled mindlessly.

Dan jerked his thumb towards Madam Rosa's doorway. 'Well, he's quite safe in there so why not come on the ghost train with us?'

'I've done that.'

'The dodgems, then.'

'Done that too. Anyway, I'd rather wait for Jim.' I

mounted the first step to give me the advantage of height.

Dan stepped closer. 'I was coming to see you earlier. Lucky I didn't, eh?'

'Yeah. You'd have had a wasted trip, wouldn't you?'

'Come on, Nell.' He gave me another of the famous winks. 'Let's have a bit of fun.'

'No thanks.'

'You're not mad at me for not calling you last week, are you? I was busy, see.'

'Behind the bar at the Feathers, I suppose?'

We eyed each other across hostile territory.

Dan shrugged. 'So I didn't get the job. So what?'

'So you never applied for it in the first place because Archie Stobbs had it all buttoned up. So what was the point?'

His face reddened. To tell the truth, I felt quite sorry for him. The gang were staring at him as if they couldn't believe their ears.

'Well, you were fooled, weren't you?' he said, grinning round at his mates. 'You should have seen the look on your face.'

'You should see the look on yours now,' I said quietly.

Everyone except Dan laughed. His mouth suddenly tightened into a thin line and stepping forward he grabbed my arm and pulled me off the step. Before I could protest I was hustled outside the covered area of the fair and we were all bowling along with the crowd in the direction of the Enterprise Wheel.

'I can't go on the Wheel,' I shouted trying to shake off Dan's grip, but he was so busy arguing with Mick about who should pay for the tickets that he didn't even hear me.

We reached the stand just as the cars had stopped and people were coming off. They all looked pretty dazed. One girl moaned, 'God, I'm not going on that thing again!'

I glanced at the long arm which raised the circle of cars into the air. Suppose it broke and collapsed? We'd be stone dead in a trice.

' . . . sixty miles an hour,' someone said.

I yanked my arm free and Dan spun round. 'What's the matter with you?'

'I'm not going,' I said between clenched teeth.

He started to say something but the crowd queuing behind us suddenly surged forward and the man in charge shouted, 'Move along quickly, please. There's room for everyone. Keep moving.'

I tried to break away but I was hemmed in on all sides.

'This is the last ride for the night,' Dan said, 'that's why it's so crowded.' At least I think that's what he said. The noise was so terrific that I only caught some of the words.

I pulled at his sleeve and tried to explain that I was frightened but I seemed to have lost my voice and what with the music and the shouting I hadn't a hope of making myself understood. We were more or less shoved into a waiting car. We both sat on the same seat, Dan behind me with his arms around my waist. There were no straps or anything to hold us, but the sides of the car had horizontal bars caging us inside.

'I can't bear it,' I said burying my face in my hands.

Dan laughed. 'You'll love it when we get going.'

I groaned. 'I expect I'll be sick all over you.'

'Try it and I'll chuck you overboard.'

I knew he didn't mean it but it was enough to start

my teeth chattering with fear. Looking back, I wonder why I didn't make a break for it then and there. I can only say that I seemed to be glued to my seat, incapable of action of any kind.

The next few minutes were, without exaggeration, the worst of my life. Immediately the Wheel took off the speed rapidly increased and the great arm lifted us into the air until we were flying in a circle upside down over the fair with its blur of lights and sea of white, upturned faces. The wind whistled in my ears and whipped my hair about my head. The stars seemed very close and I suddenly realized that it was dark. I tried to keep my eyes closed but I couldn't help looking down. It seemed as though every moment I'd be hurled to the ground and smashed to a pulp. A terrific pressure had gathered in the top of my skull and I could hardly breathe.

'I must get out,' I moaned grabbing the bars of the car.

'Don't be stupid,' Dan said in my ear. 'It will soon be over.'

'No! I must get out now! Now, do you hear?' And using all my strength I wriggled and struggled to free myself from the strange force that pinned me to my seat. Dan hung grimly on to my waist and the Wheel spun dizzily and all I could hear was the howling wind punctuated by distant shrieks and wails and gales of mad laughter. At one point I thought I must be in hell and turning to glance at Dan saw his teeth bared in a frightening devilish grin. Once I thought I saw Jim among the faces in the crowd below and I shouted his name but when we slowed down and stopped he was nowhere to be seen.

I couldn't move. I mean I literally couldn't move, so

Dan had to scoop me up in his arms and stagger out of the car and down the steps holding me like a sack of potatoes. He put me down near the perimeter fence and I was promptly sick. Boy was I sick – hamburgers, ice-cream, the lot. The gang tottered up two by two, chuckling appreciatively about the ride but they soon faded when they saw me puking my heart up. Dan, to give him his due, did what he could to help. He even produced a glass of water from somewhere.

'Honest to God, Nell, I didn't know you'd react like that,' he said guiltily. 'Why didn't you say something?'

I stared at him in dumb amazement. Why hadn't I . . .? Oh well, no point in raking it over now.

'I want Jim,' I said groggily.

Dan looked around. 'Yeah. Well you just sit there and relax and I'll go find him.'

He disappeared, leaving me sitting on the ground, empty and giddy and light-headed with relief. It had been a nightmare but it was over. If you'd asked me about it beforehand I'd have said an experience like that would send me out of my mind but – and this was the news of the year – it hadn't and here I was, sick as a dog, but otherwise none the worse for wear. Amazing. I must have reserves of strength that I knew nothing about.

'Well, I've looked everywhere but I can't find him,' Dan said when he came back.

I groaned. 'But he must be somewhere. He can't still be with Madam Rosa.'

'No, she's shut up shop for the night.' He grinned. 'Perhaps Jim never left the caravan.'

'Don't be daft!' I said crossly. 'Are you sure you looked properly?'

'Course I did. Anyway, the crowd's thinned out now

so he'd be easy to spot.'

'But how am I going to get back to Finchings?' I wailed.

'I'll take you, of course. I always do, don't I?'

Yes, I thought, but things are different now.

'I haven't got a crash helmet,' I said looking desperately round for the missing Jim.

Dan clucked impatiently. 'You know I always carry a spare. Come on, Nell. Everyone's going now. If we stay much longer they'll ask us to help with the cleaning up.'

It was true. We were the only people not connected with the fair still hanging around.

'I just can't think what's happened to him,' I said anxiously as we walked through the dimmed fairground past the closed stalls and silent dodgems.

'Who cares?' Dan said, draping his arm around my neck.

It was all I could do not to turn on him and tell him just where to get off. After all, he'd neglected me for days; then when I was enjoying myself with Jim he'd dragged me away and put me through that torture, yet he seemed to think things were the same as usual between us. How insensitive can you get?

He lent me his jacket for the drive back to Finchings; even so by the time we arrived I was cold. It was well past midnight and my country nose told me there would be rain before morning.

Dan stopped the bike inside the gates and slid to the ground.

'You can take me up to the house.' I said, staying put on the seat.

'You're in a hurry suddenly.'

'Yeah I am, as a matter of fact.'

'A few more minutes won't hurt.'

'No thanks.'

'What's bitten you, then? You still angry about the fair?'

'No.'

'Well, is it about last week? Me staying away and all that?'

'You could have telephoned or something but I'm over it now.'

'So what's it all about?'

It was obviously crunch time. 'I don't want to go out with you any more,' I said calmly.

'You *are* mad at me. I thought so.'

'No I'm not. I just don't think we have enough in common. I mean we don't have anything to say to each other.'

He gave an exaggerated sigh. 'You're always on about talking. There are better things to do than talk.'

'Such as?'

He gave a cheeky grin. 'Come here and I'll show you.'

'Oh, Dan!' I said furiously. 'You'll never change, will you?'

'It's that ape Jim Blair, isn't it? You've fallen for him. I knew it when I saw you both at the fair. Why that sneaky son of a . . .'

'Dan, I must go in now,' I said quickly. 'If Jane's up she'll be worried about me.'

He stepped back from the bike and folded his arms. 'Off you go then. No one's stopping you.'

I peered apprehensively up the dark drive. 'Aren't you going to take me?'

His mouth drooped sullenly. 'Why the hell should I?'

'Okay,' I said sliding off the seat. 'Then I'll walk.'

'No you don't.' He shoved me on to the seat again. 'I suppose I'll have to drive you. I don't want someone to find your battered corpse in the ditch tomorrow and lay the blame on me.'

I grinned gratefully. 'Thanks, Dan.'

'Oh anytime,' he said getting on the bike. 'Just anytime. After all, I run a free taxi service for all my ex-birds, don't I?'

Jane and Bill were waiting for me in the doorway of the house, looking tired and cross. They were both in their night clothes.

'Where the devil have you been?' Bill asked roughly. 'You said you'd be back at a reasonable hour. Do you call one in the morning reasonable?'

'No but . . .'

'That looked like Dan Glease driving away. I thought you set out with Jim Blair.'

'I did but there was a bit of a mix up . . .'

'So that's what they call it these days is it?'

'No honestly you don't understand . . .'

'Oh do stop it, Bill,' Jane said, smothering a yawn. 'She's back now and that's all that matters. Nell, we've been worried about you so naturally we're a bit upset.'

'I'm sorry,' I said. 'I really am. You see it wasn't my fault.'

'Oh no, of course not!' Bill sneered.

'I am sure it wasn't,' Jane said soothingly. 'Anyway, we can all relax now.'

'That bloody Glease boy,' Bill fumed. 'I'll have his guts for garters one day!'

'Bill!' Jane raised a pacifying hand. 'Nell's tired and we're tired so why don't we all go to bed?'

'Hmph!' Bill stomped off into the house, his slippers

flapping on the gravel. Almost immediately he stuck his head outside again. 'If she goes on like this she'll have to go home,' he growled. 'After all, she's not yet seventeen and we are responsible for her.'

I drew myself up to my full height. 'I think you should address me in person,' I said. 'After all, I'm not the cat's mother or something.'

And with that I stalked off to my own bed over the stable-yard.

Chapter 14

I'm afraid I didn't make it downstairs until after nine the next morning. Naturally I apologized to Jane who was getting the kids ready for a bean-picking expedition to the kitchen garden.

She gave me a concerned look. 'You're a bit peaky today, Nell. Are you all right?'

'Sure,' I said, tying a double bow in Roddy's trainer laces.

'Right. Off we go, then. I'll carry the orange squash and you bring the children.'

We shepherded our little flock outside and up the hill to the walled garden. Plod came with us, leaping and barking and generally making a fool of himself.

'By the way,' Jane said, thrusting open the door with the faded 'private' sign on it, 'Jim called before breakfast with the eggs. He wanted to make sure you got home okay. He said you disappeared at the fair but then he saw you with Dan so he knew you'd be all right.'

'Did he leave a message for me?'

'No. You didn't really expect him to, did you? Personally I thought it was rather noble of him to come and enquire about you.'

'I suppose so.'

To be honest, I was feeling a teeny bit resentful that he hadn't made a greater effort to find me at the fair but Jane had just explained the whole thing. If Jim had seen me with Dan he must have thought I'd gone of my own accord, preferring his company to Jim's. What a muddle! I must go in search of him soon and tell him what really happened. But when? I was on duty until after supper so it would have to wait until then.

Picking beans with a batch of handicapped kids can be a frustrating business, especially if your mind's not on the job.

Matthew of the one arm (otherwise known as the one-armed bandit) kept making off with the trug basket and Plod insisted on digging up onions and Philip and Mary ('the terrible twins') kept chasing chickens — but eventually everyone settled down to their various small jobs while Jane and I picked beans and kept a weather eye on our charges.

Of course I was expecting her to say something more about last night, and after a bit she did.

'Must have been quite a party to start with one guy and end up with another.'

'My fatal charm,' I said, hoping to laugh it off. No such luck.

'Jim seemed a bit put out this morning,' she went on. 'Not that he said anything, of course, but you know our Jim when he goes all stern and silent.'

I did.

'It was awful,' I said. 'You see, we were having a really great time until . . .' I stopped mid-sentence, suddenly recalling the moment outside Madam Rosa's when, in a flash, I'd discovered that Jim meant something special in my life and I'd had this premonition that if he went inside the caravan it would all go wrong for us.

'Well?' Jane asked, eyeing me through the bean-row. 'What happened?'

Normally I resent being questioned like that but Jane had been kind and I trusted her and, in a way, she had a right to know, so I gave her a potted version of my night at the fair.

When I'd finished she said, 'Look, Nell, it's none of my business but if I could choose between Jim Blair and Dan Glease I know who'd get my vote.'

I shrugged. 'You may be right,' I said and I wandered off to find out where Matthew had hidden the trug. I mean, no one's going to dictate who my boyfriend will be. Not even Jane.

After we'd picked the beans we sat in the shade and handed round mugs of orange squash and some biscuits. The kids then started to play a funny little game of their own while Jane and I lolled under an old apple tree and watched them.

'What are you going to do with your life?' Jane asked suddenly. 'Have you thought about it?'

I chewed the end of a bean. 'Not really.'

'How much longer have you got at school?'

'That depends. I can leave now if I want.'

'Don't you like school?'

I hesitated. It was just the moment to tell her about Mum, my illness, my home tutor and my decision not to return to school but somehow it all seemed remote and unimportant. In my heart I knew it was neither but I just didn't want to talk about it. Frankly I didn't want to think about anything except how soon I could find Jim and explain about last night.

Jane didn't press me to reply – she was good about things like that. She just said, 'Well, if you ever feel like chatting about it I'd be glad to lend an ear. As a matter of fact Bill and I have been wondering if you'd ever thought about training to teach handicapped children.'

'Oh.' I blushed. Fancy their talking about me like that behind my back! I felt quite pleased. 'Don't you have to have A levels and stuff?' I asked.

'I expect so. You'd have to find out. But that wouldn't be a problem for you, would it?'

'N-no.'

A levels? I wasn't even planning to take Os. A fat chance I had of becoming a teacher! Now if it hadn't been for Mark's treachery . . . Closing my eyes against the dazzle on the greenhouse roof I tried to summon up his face: his blue eyes, his grin, the way he ran his hand through his blond hair – but I couldn't. He seemed as out of focus as everything else I'd left behind in Hobleigh. I heaved a small sigh. You couldn't hold on to anything for long. Even the determination to get my own back by denying the world my brilliant future no longer gave me the bitter pleasure it once had.

'Well, I'll think about it,' I said. After all, if a person takes the trouble to suggest something serious like that the least you can do is promise to consider it, even if you know it's impossible.

What with one thing and another Marion and I hadn't

managed to get together for a good jaw since the fateful day I'd hacked off her hair. I say 'fateful' because that's just what it turned out to be. Within a week, believe it or not, she'd acquired a proper boy-friend. His name was Jasper (honest!), known to his intimates as Jaz, and he worked in the off-licence in the street behind the Gleases' house. Marion got to know him when she popped in to replenish her mother's weekly supply of lager but he never asked her out or anything. Anyway, a couple of days after the trans-formation scene she went in as usual and he couldn't take his eyes off her. In fact he asked her to go to the flicks with him that evening. That's really all I knew. Whenever I saw her she looked bright-eyed and bushy-tailed and every other word was Jaz so I just nodded and grinned and waited for her to come down from cloud nine.

When Jane and I got back from bean-picking Marion was supervising the hand-washing routine before lunch. I saw immediately that something was wrong and I assumed she'd had a row with Jaz, but she denied it.

'It's Nick,' she said. 'He won't get out of bed.'

I laughed. 'Wait till he's hungry.'

But she didn't laugh with me. 'No, it's serious, Nell. He just lies with his face to the wall and won't speak to anyone. Mum's doing her nut. Even the doctor can't get any sense out of him.'

I dropped on to my knees to dry the hands of our youngest child, Penny. Penny had violet eyes and corn coloured curls but she'd suffered brain damage during an illness soon after she was born and she hadn't developed mentally beyond the toddler stage. While patting her little hands dry I couldn't help thinking how lucky Nick was to be alive and relatively un-damaged after his accident. He could so easily have been reduced to a state worse even than Penny's. He ought to come to Finchings and see these kids, then he might understand and be thankful.

Penny suddenly smiled, her eyes sparkling with mischief, and leaning forward she yanked at the silver chain I wore around my neck. It broke and she held it up, cooing with pleasure. How could I be cross?

'Shall I talk to Nick?' I asked Marion. 'I think he quite likes me.'

'You can if you like,' she said, 'but I think you'll find it hard going.'

'Would your Mum mind?'

'No. She's at her wit's end. Anyway, she thinks you're great.'

'Okay. I'll come as soon as I can.'

Penny chortled and stuck her finger up my nostril. Honestly, kids!

After supper I slipped away to my room and changed into a blue-and-white striped skirt and shirt that I'd been saving for a special occasion. It wasn't a special occasion but I wanted to look my best when I arrived on Jim's doorstep to explain about the fair.

Jane was bent over the accounts and Bill was watching telly when I put my head around the study door.

'I'm off to see Jim,' I said.

They exchanged glances. 'Nell, are you sure . . . ' Jane began.

'Oh let her go,' Bill said turning back to the telly.

Jane shrugged helplessly.

'I won't be long,' I promised.

'We've heard that before,' Bill muttered as I closed the door.

Honestly, if he was going to act like my jailer just because I'd come in late one night I'd have to . . . well I'd certainly have to . . . but I never got around to thinking what I'd do because at that moment a drop of rain splashed on to my nose followed, faster and faster, by other drops. I began running down the back drive which led to the rear entrance of the estate as fast as my legs could carry me. By the time I pushed open the Blairs' gate it was pelting down and ducking under their porch I knocked on the door and waited, listening to the steady beat of the rain on the leaves and watching puddles form on the dusty path. There's something nice about rain after a long dry spell. It releases all kinds of delicious smells and makes everything seem bright and new. I was quite happy leaning against the wall for a minute or two. I knew they were at home because I could hear low voices arguing inside. Anyway, it was Mr Blair who opened the door in the end. He didn't seem too surprised at seeing me.

'Hallo, Nell. You look wet, girl.'

'It wasn't raining when I set out, Mr Blair.'

'Hm. That so? We certainly need the rain.' He gazed over my head at the downpour. 'We certainly do.'

I nodded. 'It'll be good for the veg won't it? The beans and that?'

'Oh yes. It'll set the beans all right.' He chuckled. 'Save me doing the watering, eh?'

Wasn't he ever going to ask me in?

'Well, er . . . could I see Jim, Mr Blair?'

'Jim?' He glanced over his shoulder. 'I'm not too sure what he's doing just now.'

'I'll only keep him a minute. It's rather important.'

'Important, is it?' At last he stepped aside. 'Then you'd better come in and get dry. I'll see if I can find him.'

I crossed the threshold and he closed the door. Two glasses of beer stood on the table and the telly performed silently in a corner . . . I'd obviously interrupted a cosy family evening.

Mr Blair plodded across to the inner door, lifted the latch and opened it a fraction. 'Jim? Er . . . Nell's here.'

I could tell he was embarrassed because, while we waited, he rocked backwards and forwards on his feet and whistled quietly through his teeth.

Then the door opened and Jim stood there, still in his working clothes. He had an enormous bruise on his left cheek and the area around his left eye was badly swollen and turning blue.

'You wanted to see me?' he said coldly.

'Yeah . . .' I was so shocked by his appearance that I totally forgot why I'd come. 'What on earth has . . ?' I began but he cut me short.

'Never mind about that. What do you want?'

'I – I came to explain about . . . ' I shot an embarrassed look at Mr Blair who was still rocking backwards and forwards, looking utterly miserable. ' . . . about last night,' I finished lamely.

He came further into the room. 'There's no need.'

'But I want to.'

'I'd rather you didn't.'

'I think I'll just er . . .' Mr Blair mumbled sliding out of the door.

'Jim, it really wasn't my fault.'

'I'm sure it wasn't. Anyway, you're free to do what you want. Okay?'

'Yeah but . . .'

'Look, forget it, will you?'

'But I haven't told you what happened.'

'Words often just make things worse. The whole episode is over. Right?'

I sighed unhappily. 'Okay, if you say so.'

'Right. That's that, then. Was there anything else?'

I shook my head, afraid to speak in case I burst into stupid tears. Why wouldn't he let me explain? Why wouldn't he listen? What had he done to his face? A hundred questions were running through my mind as we stood there glaring at each other, listening to the rain drumming against the windows. If there had been the slightest softening of his expression I'd have had another go at explaining. But there wasn't. He looked as hard and unyielding as if he were chiselled out of flintstone – except for the angry red glint in his good eye. Shocked by its ferocity I suddenly thought – he hates me – and I made a dive for the front door and fumbled clumsily with the stiff latch.

'You'd better wait until the rain stops,' Jim said. His voice may have been a fraction less chilly. I don't know. I was beyond caring.

'No thanks,' I croaked, practically choking on the words. 'I wouldn't stay a minute longer if you paid me!' And yanking open the door I splashed wildly down the muddy path, blinded by tears which the rain washed away as fast as they overflowed. By the time I reached Finchings my shoes were filled with water and my special-occasion dress clung to my body like an old floorcloth and my head raged at the whole goddam rotten world and Jim Blair in particular.

Chapter 15

I hadn't the least desire to see Dan so soon after breaking with him, but I'd promised Marion that I'd talk to Nick, so on my afternoon off I again found myself (with some misgivings) knocking at the Gleases' front door. Mrs Glease opened it. She looked thinner and had dark circles under her eyes.

'Hallo. I've just put on the kettle. Fancy a cuppa?'

'Yeah. Thanks.' I followed her into the kitchen. Lettuces and hard-boiled eggs covered the table.

'By the end of the summer I never want to see another lettuce or another lodger,' she said giving the salad spinner a violent twist of the wrist.

I sat down and began to shell the eggs, piling them into a blue-and-white striped bowl. 'Go on,' I teased. 'You love it really. You're a natural in this business, Mrs Glease, because you like people. Imagine the summer with nothing to do. You'd go spare.'

Getting down the cups from their shelf she poured our tea. 'I suppose you're right, Nell. It's all this worry over Nick that's making me feel bad. I can't concentrate on anything else and I feel so tired all the time.'

She looked tired, too. Her normally springy hair was in need of a wash and her chubby face seemed to sag, revealing lines I hadn't noticed before.

'He's no better, then?'

She shook her head sadly. 'It's been five days now. We can't do anything with him. He just lies there.'

'Is he eating okay?'

'I suppose so. He shoves the empty tray outside his door so he must be. I've taken away the key of his room because he kept locking himself in.'

'What does the doctor say?'

She stirred another spoonful of sugar into her tea. That made the fourth.

'He's as baffled as we are. Can't find a thing wrong. Even his poor old legs are coming along fine. I'm so afraid this mood – or whatever it is – will last into September and he'll refuse to go to school again. We'll have real trouble with the education people if he does. They have warned him but he won't listen.'

I sipped my tea thoughtfully, my mind darting hither and thither in search of a clue to Nick's latest problem.

'Did anything particular happen the day before he took to his bed?' I asked.

'I don't think so.'

'I mean did he seem exactly the same as usual?'

She frowned in an effort to remember. 'Well, let's see. He came down late and had his breakfast in the front room to get away from the mess in the kitchen. I was busy doing the rooms so I didn't see him again until twelve when Dan came in and we all had a snack.' Her expression suddenly changed, becoming, I thought, a trifle wary. 'By the way, Dan's not in. Did you want to see him specially?'

I kept careful control of my face and voice. 'Oh no. I came to see Nick. Marion's working this afternoon and she suggested I pop round and have a chat with him.'

'That's nice of you – not that you'll get much change

115

out of him. So you haven't seen Dan lately?'

'Not since Saturday,' I said cheerfully.

She nodded. 'I just wondered because . . .'

'Back to Nick,' I said quickly. 'What happened that afternoon? Can you remember?'

'Nothing much. I went shopping and when I came back he'd gone to his room. All I know is he's been there ever since.'

I drained my cup and stared down at the tea leaves. Mum used to claim that she saw things – people, money, illness, etc. in the leaves. Dad and I used to scoff, of course, but it was weird the way she got things right. Perhaps the gift had percolated through to me. I concentrated on the leaves but instead of forming a pattern they had clumped together in a solid box-like mass.

'What does Nick usually do with himself in the afternoons?' I asked. 'He must have a routine of sorts.'

'Oh he does,' she said drily. 'He watches telly. His whole life is spent watching telly. It's a wonder he isn't square-eyed.'

Telly. The tea-leaf box in my cup! Of course. It had to be right.

I leapt up from the table. 'Do you take the TV guides?'

'Yes.'

'Where are last week's?'

She looked vaguely around. 'In the sitting room I expect.'

'Do you mind if I look?'

'Help yourself.'

I crossed the hall into the family sitting room. The current guides were on the table but the old ones were in the rack and pulling them out I turned to last

Friday's programmes. After studying them carefully I replaced them and walked thoughtfully upstairs.

Stepping over a tray of empty dishes, I knocked gently on Nick's door. There was no answer, so I went in. The curtains were drawn but a ray of sunlight had found a way through and lay in a golden bar across the dark figure on the bed. His back was towards me and his shoulders looked pathetically thin under his striped pyjamas. His hair obviously hadn't been combed for days and stood on end, giving his head a hedgehog-like appearance.

'Nick? It's me – Nell. Can I come in?'

His shoulders gave a slight convulsive movement that might have been a shrug but he didn't reply. I walked to the foot of the bed and looked at him lengthways, so to speak. 'Dan and I have broken up,' I said. I don't know why I came out with it like that – perhaps because I wanted to make him a present of something personal in order to get something personal in return. He didn't move but he squinted down his nose at me.

'It was last Saturday,' I said. 'I just told him I didn't want to see him any more.'

Silence. His gaze moved away from me, back to the wall. I walked over to the window, enticed by the bright beam thrusting between the curtains and the light and life outside this oppressive little room.

'Then why are you here?'

Startled, I spun round. He hadn't moved but he'd definitely spoken. What I said next would be vitally important because it would carry the seeds for the rest of our conversation. The trouble was I couldn't think what to say. Then quite suddenly I didn't want to say anything at all. After all, what right had I to intrude on his unhappiness? Why should he be 'cured' if he wasn't ready? Why should I, or anyone, interfere with his way of coping with his troubles?

'I don't know,' I said sadly. 'I had an idea that I could help you or something but I guess I can't, so I think I'll go.' With that I went to the door and opened it.

'Nell. Wait . . .'

I looked back. He was sitting up in bed looking at me with large pleading eyes. I closed the door again and leaned back against it.

'I know why you're here,' I said quietly. 'You watched that telly programme on Friday afternoon about Lilleshall, didn't you? You saw them all tearing around doing marvellous things – things you could have done just as well if not better – and you heard the coaches saying what a brilliant lot of lads they were, the stars of the future etc. And you thought – it's not fair; I could have been one of them if I hadn't broken my legs – but there was no one to blame except yourself. So that's who you blamed and punished – yourself. I just bet your mum used to send you to your room when you were a little kid and you'd done something wrong. Am I right?'

He flung himself down again, turned on to his stomach and buried his face in the pillow.

I shoved his clothes off the chair by the bed and sat down. 'Look, it's awful for you, Nick. I know it's awful. It's been a terrible time, what with your dad and everything. Marion says he was a great guy.'

He twisted his head towards me and I saw tears on his cheeks.

'Dad *was* great,' he said hoarsely. 'Why did he have to snuff it? We needed him. I needed him. He was a great coach and he had faith in me. He was quite strict about my training but I didn't mind. In fact I enjoyed it. I don't understand. One moment he was running beside me and the next he was . . .'

I waited but he couldn't go on. 'Nick' — I leaned forward but tried to keep the urgency I felt out of my voice ' — you surely don't think it was your fault that your dad died? You can't think that?'

'He was too old to run about like he did,' he said, his voice muffled in the pillow. 'We used to run together as part of my training. He always came along. He seemed so fit. I never thought — ' He stopped, suddenly seized with silent, racking sobs. A dog barked in the street and a man swore at it. A bee droned somewhere in the room. The air felt heavy with guilt and sorrow.

'It's hard when they go,' I said gently. 'My mum went three years ago. She may be dead. I just don't know. But I do know that I felt guilty and lonely and totally scared. I had a sort of nervous breakdown. They nearly put me in the local bin for a spell.'

He pushed himself up on one elbow, tears still dripping off his chin. 'I thought your mum died in a car accident.'

I shrugged. 'Telling people that is easier than telling them she did a bunk because she didn't like me and Dad enough to stay. I'm not very brave, I guess.'

He wiped his nose and eyes with the sleeve of his pyjamas. 'So what happened to you afterwards?'

'I didn't want to see people any more – my friends and that – and I stayed away from school because every time I went there I got sick.'

'Like me.'

'Sort of like you. Anyway, in the end they gave me a home tutor. He taught me for three years but I'm supposed to go back to school next term to do my Os.'

Curiosity glinted behind the tears. 'And will you go?'

'I guess so. You see I need what they can give me.' Was that me speaking? I could hardly believe my own ears. Until that very moment I had had no intention of going back. Or I had *thought* I had no intention. What had taken place in my mind to make me voice a decision I didn't even know I'd made? Not that the process mattered – I could sort that out later – the important thing was Nick.

By this time he was sitting up in bed. 'Won't it be difficult, going back after so long?'

I nodded. 'Yeah.'

'Then why do it? You're over sixteen. You can leave if you want.'

'What then? I'd have no qualifications and you know how difficult it is to get a job. What would I do?'

He lifted his thin shoulders. 'Dunno. Bum around, I suppose – like Dan.'

'Big deal!'

'If you go back, your friends will probably think you are still a nutter.'

'Does it matter what they think?'

He looked shocked. 'Of course. They are your mates, aren't they?'

'Is that why you won't go back? Because in your mates' eyes you won't be the big man you were before the accident?'

He flushed and looked away. 'Course not. I can't go back because my legs are still bad. I have to use a stick.'

I shook my head. 'Come off it, Nick. That doesn't mean you can't use your head to learn. Believe it or not, there are other things in life besides playing football.'

'Such as?' he said gloomily.

'I dunno. You'll have to find out for yourself but you

won't do it lying in this dark smelly room. Can I at least pull the curtains?'

He didn't say no so I got up and let in the sunlight, then I leaned on the sill and watched Mrs Glease chatting to her neighbour over the hedge. She was obviously talking about Nick because she glanced up and saw me. I waved and smiled then I turned back into the room. Something very important still had to be said and Nick had to believe it. But was he ready? Had he punished himself enough?

'Of course,' I said slowly,' I wasn't responsible for Mum's flit any more than you were for your dad's death. My mum had just had enough and your dad well . . .he just died, didn't he?'

He sighed deeply. 'I dunno. All that running at his age . . .'

'No,' I said firmly. 'He just died. The buzzer went. His time was up. Okay?'

Silence.

'He'd probably have gone just as quickly if he'd sat around watching telly all day. Quicker in fact.'

Silence.

I stretched and yawned. 'Well, I've had enough of the stink in here so I think I'll go for a swim before I catch the bus back to Finchings.'

'Why did you break with Dan?' he asked suddenly.

I opened the door. 'Because I'm sick of the fruit-machines in the amusement arcade. See you around, okay?'

'Okay.' He swung his legs over the side of the bed and reached for his jeans. 'Tell you something, Nell. I'm not going back to school next term. They'll have to carry me there first.'

Oh well, I thought, running downstairs, you can't win 'em all.

At the bottom of the stairs I almost ran slap into Dan. He had a swollen nose and looked as if he'd been in a fight. A fight? Oh no! He brushed past me without speaking and I stared after him in utter dismay, then I fled the house without even saying goodbye to Mrs Glease.

Chapter 16

The shock of seeing Dan like that banished all thought of swimming. Instead I made directly for the bus stop, my thoughts in a turmoil. Dan's swollen nose and Jim's battered face kept reappearing in my mind's eye. Could they have got into a fight together? If not, it was an amazing coincidence. If they had, it must have been because of Saturday night at the fair. Anyway, there was nothing I could do about it so I forced the mystery to the back of my mind and turned my thoughts to Nick.

I'd been right about the telly programme. He'd watched it on Friday afternoon, seen with his own eyes what he was missing at Lilleshall and, overcome with self-pity, had shut himself into his room to wallow in misery. But I hadn't realized, until he said something about his dad's training with him that, to add to his troubles, he blamed himself for his dad's heart attack. I'd done my best to convince him that he was in no way responsible but had I succeeded? Anyway, if I'd done no more than bring the bedroom seige to an end, at least Mrs Glease's problems would be slightly eased.

As for my own decision to return to school, on reflection it was really quite simple. I had been intrigued by Jane's suggestion that I might train to teach handicapped children. I enjoyed the children. When one of them achieved something beyond our expectations I was really glad and I wanted the kid to go on and stun me with some other marvel. In the few weeks I had been at Finchings I had discovered that I had amazing reserves of tolerance and patience. I could sit for hours playing idiotic games or showing a child how to tie a shoe-lace. I'd become expert at spotting trouble and doing something to dispel it. In other words, I seemed to fit in. Of course it was often boring but Jane and Bill had been so good about giving me time off that I'd never felt trapped. If I could get my Os and then a couple of As – or whatever exam the Minister of Education thought to impose upon us at the time – I would be qualified to do a proper training. On the other hand, if I quit school now and Jane and Bill were ever forced to close – for health reasons or anything – I would be left high and dry with nothing but a little experience to help me get another job. And I did not want to 'bum around like Dan', as Nick so graphically put it.

Amazing to think that my time at Finchings was nearly up. Already the trees were showing signs of turning and the fierce midsummer heat had gone out of the sun. The weeks had flown. It had all been lovely and it had looked like getting even lovelier, but something had gone wrong . . .

*

When I shut the front door Bill rushed out of his study looking more harassed than usual.

'Nell! Thank God you're back!'

'Why? What's up? Is it one of the kids?' My mind flew to Rachel, who wasn't well again.

'No, it's not that. It's . . . Nell . . . ' He sat on the oak settle in front of the huge empty fireplace and patted the place beside him. He looked so grim that I sat down at once.

'Now I want you to tell me the truth,' he said seriously. 'Did your mother really die in an accident?'

'M-Mum?' I stammered. 'Why?'

He shook his head irritably. 'Come on, Nell. Let's have it.'

I swallowed. 'Er . . . well, she might have. I don't know.'

'So what happened?'

'She left home suddenly,' I mumbled. 'I don't know more than that.' Suddenly I felt an embarrassed burst of anger. 'Look, what's all this about? Why the third degree?'

His pale eyes searched my face for some clue to help us both.

'Because she's here,' he said quietly. 'That's why.'

She was sitting next to Jane on the sofa in the drawing-room. They both got up as we came in and Jane walked quickly over to me, briefly touched my arm, then left the room with Bill. I spun round in a panic, but they'd gone, so I turned reluctantly back again.

'Hallo Nell,' Mum said, exhaling a cloud of cigarette smoke. 'You've changed. Grown up and that.'

'Yeah.' I stared at her. I just couldn't think what to say and, oddly, I didn't feel a thing. Before, when I'd imagined this moment, I'd seen us throwing ourselves into each other's arms sobbing with joy, etc., instead of which here we were, ten metres apart, acting like wary strangers.

'Come over here then and let's have a proper look at you,' she said.

I walked over to the sofa and we both sat down. She'd changed all right – never mind about me. In spite of the expertly applied make-up she looked older. Her hair was now short and straight and a brighter blonde than I remembered. She was wearing a kind of street gear – white jacket and trousers with a satin top which made her look like she was trying to be young or something. The ash tray beside her was full of fag ends. That at least hadn't changed.

'You're happy here?' she asked.

'Yeah. It's okay.'

'That Mrs Whatsit seems to like you. They were a bit stunned to see me, though.' She uttered a short, staccato laugh. 'What on earth had you told them about me?'

'That you were dead.'

She looked startled. 'Dead? Why did you tell them that?'

'For all I knew you were.'

This seemed to unsettle her because she took a long drag of her ciggy and her eyelids flickered nervously.

'Yeah, well. I suppose I should have got in touch but I thought you'd settle down better with Dad if I didn't.'

'Thoughtful of you.'

She reached out and took one of my hands. 'Don't be mean, love. I've missed you.'

I'd forgotten how cold her hands were. Small cold claws. I withdrew my own hand gently.

'Why are you here, Mum?'

'I work in an antique market in Bournemouth and that Mrs Lawton from the village came in yesterday . . .' (Pause for another staccato laugh.) 'I must say she nearly fainted when she recognized me. Anyway, she told me where you were so I thought we'd better meet again. I hoped it would be a nice surprise.'

A nice surprise? This time I felt like laughing. She made it sound as though she'd returned early from a holiday or something.

She stubbed out her fag and immediately extracted another from her bag. 'I must say you don't seem too pleased to see me. Mrs Lawton said you'd been ill but you look okay to me. Blooming, in fact. So what was wrong?'

'I'm fine now,' I said. I mean what was the point of going into all that when she obviously hadn't the least idea of the havoc she'd caused.

There was a short silence.

'How's your dad?'

'Okay. Now.'

'What do you mean, now?'

'He was in a pretty bad way when you didn't turn up or write or anything.'

'Was he? Wonders'll never cease!'

'Mum! He's not that bad.'

She had the grace to look slightly shamefaced.

'No. Well, as I say, I thought it would make things easier in the long run. Better for everyone, you know.'

This was too much. 'Better for who?' I snapped. 'Better for you perhaps. Certainly not better for us.'

'It was difficult. You know how things were between your dad and me.'

'I *don't* know. I was just a kid of thirteen. You were

126

my mum and dad. Home was home. Of course I knew you didn't get along too well. So what? Millions of couples don't get on. Most of my friends' parents don't get on. It's known as the Human Condition or something. How was I to know you were planning the Great Escape?'

She gazed at me with astonishment. 'You sound so bitter, Nell. I never thought you'd be bitter. I missed you a lot and I often wanted to write but I thought Dad would trace me and try to get me back. I suppose it was cowardly but I just couldn't face any more of those god-awful scenes.'

'Who made the scenes, Mother?'

It was the first time I'd called her that. It sounded so odd that I got up and walked over to the windows.

'Now don't you start in on me,' she said sharply. 'It took quite a lot of courage to come here, you know. It won't take much to leave.'

'Then why don't you?' Outside, Jane's precious double dahlias were waving about in the breeze like a lot of blowsy tarts.

'Jack said you'd be like this.'

I leaned my forehead against the window. Such a pity the roses were over. 'Who's Jack?'

'The man I'm going to marry. You'll like him. He restores antique furniture and that. He's very kind and he's mad about me.'

I looked round at her. 'So you're not going back to Dad?'

'Oh no.' She sounded surprised. 'You didn't think I would, did you?'

'Not really.' But of course I had. Briefly, in the immediate shock of seeing her again, I had even envisaged us all sitting around the kitchen table like we used to: Dad silent behind his paper, Mum and I chatting about this and that. Now that I knew it would never happen, my overriding feeling, strangely, was one of relief. Since she had gone the house had been relatively peaceful. Her restless spirit no longer dominated our lives. We'd grown used to her absence.

'Do you think he'll make trouble over the divorce?' she asked, with just a hint of nervousness in her voice.

'I shouldn't think so.'

She gave a long sigh of relief. 'It seems funny talking to you like this. Like a grown-up person.'

'I am grown-up. I had to grow up pretty fast.'

'I suppose so. I used to think about you and wonder whether you were pretty and who was helping you buy nice clothes and . . .'

. . .And teach me about sex and talk to me about death and put their arms around me when I was miserable, I thought, listening to her ramble sentimentally on. No point in saying anything, though. She'd never understand what I'd missed, what she'd missed, what we'd all missed. Her mind was on clothes and parties and meals in smart restaurants. Oh yes, on 'Jack' too. Now she was telling me how great he was and how they'd furnished a room in their flat specially for me so that I could go and live with them.

'You'll even have your own bathroom, Nell — Jack's doing very well, you know — and we'll give you a key so you can come and go as you please. Better than a council house in Hobleigh any day! Bournemouth's a lively place, whatever they say about bath-chairs and that. You'll have lots of fun.'

'What about my education?'

'You're sixteen, aren't you? You can leave school now. Jack says he'll train you and then you can work for him. You'll like the antique business. Play your cards right and there's good money in it.'

'What about Dad?'

'Dad? What do you mean?'

'What happens to him if I go?'

She shrugged. 'He'll be okay. He's a loner. He doesn't really want anyone else around. Never has. He should have stayed single. His mother tried to warn me but then she always hated me because I was too pretty. Too popular. Too many boys were after me. I expect . . .' Curiosity gleamed in her green eyes. ' . . . they're after you now?'

I felt a flicker of positive dislike.

'Nell . . .' She got up and came over to me. 'What are you thinking? I never knew what you and your dad were thinking.'

'I'm thinking,' I said slowly, 'about a boy who thought he was responsible for his dad's heart attack. He wasn't, of course.'

She recoiled slightly. 'That's a funny thing to be thinking right now. Morbid.'

'Not really.' I looked at her standing by my side. She was now shorter than I. It felt odd to be looking down at her. 'I thought I was to blame when you went off like that,' I said. 'After all, most of the rows you had were about me.'

She appeared mystified. 'But it had nothing to do with you, love. In fact you were the main reason I stayed for so long. Anyway, soon after I left Hobleigh I met Jack. He was still married — if you could call it a marriage — so we had to go carefully until he could get things settled.'

'And then of course you didn't want everything complicated by a teenager.'

Her green eyes narrowed. 'I'm trying to be patient but that's not a very nice thing to say, Nell.'

'The truth's often nasty, Mother.'

'Cynical you are. Like your dad.'

'Maybe. That's why I'm staying with him and going back to school instead of opting for the good life with you and Jack.'

A thousand expressions flitted across her face, disbelief, anger, regret . . .

'You're passing up the opportunity of a lifetime, you know. I mean Jack's really someone in the antique world. He travels all over the place, France, Germany, the States. You could go too. You'd have a great time.'

'Yeah, well, thank him for me but I think I'll finish my education. You see, I want to teach handicapped kids.'

'You mean . . . ' She glanced around the elegant but shabbily furnished room, 'like here?'

'Maybe. I dunno. We'll have to see what turns up.'

She shook her head. 'You must be mad. Of course I'm sorry for the poor things — some of them were playing in the garden when I arrived — but you won't be giving yourself much of a chance, will you?'

'A chance for what?'

'Well there's no money in this kind of work, for a start.'

'You just don't understand.'

'Try me.'

I sighed. 'Okay. I like the kids, see? I like caring for them, helping them, teaching them. It feels right. Sorry, but I can't explain it better than that.'

She stared at me and nodded silently several times. 'You've explained it very well. Very well.' She glanced at her watch — a new one, I noticed. 'Jack said he'd bring the Jag to the gates, so I'd better go now. It'll take me about a week to walk down that drive.' She moved towards the door.

'Wait!' I said. 'I'll walk with you.'

She turned round. 'No, I'd rather go alone.' She grinned weakly. 'It isn't every day you get kicked in the teeth by your own daughter.' Her eyes filled with tears, which overflowed and spilled down her face.

Horrified I leapt across the room in a flash and wrapped my arms around her. She felt so small and thin and her hair smelt of lily-of-the-valley and stale cigarette smoke. For a moment we stood with our heads pressed together, then she shoved me away, dug out a hanky, and blew her nose.

'What a couple of nanas!' she said, grinning.

'Yeah.' I wiped away my own tears.

'You'll come and see us, then – Jack and me?'

'Of course. Soon as I can. I can't wait to use that bathroom.'

'Promise?'

'Promise.'

'Okay.' She seemed reassured. Digging in her bag she pulled out a card. 'Here's Jack's address. You can get in touch with me in the evenings.' Suddenly she thrust something crackly into my hand. 'And here's something to be going on with.'

I looked down. Fifty quid!

'It's far too much,' I gasped.

'I told you. Jack's doing well.'

'But . . .'

'Go on. Pocket it.' She darted me a strange look, half joky, half serious. 'Buy something for this dump if you like. God knows they seem to need it.'

I watched her trip jauntily down the drive, a slight, strangely unfamiliar figure with buttercup hair. My mum and yet not my mum – not as I'd known her, anyway. The restless, resentful Mum I remembered had gone for good and I didn't mind. It would be quite interesting getting to know the person who'd taken her place. And Jack, of course. Mustn't forget him. I fingered the crisp note pleasurably. I'd been wanting to buy something for Jane and Bill to remember me by and now I could.

I opened the window and leaned far out. 'Bye Mum,' I yelled.

She turned and waved, and although she was too far away for me to see her face I had the feeling that she was smiling.

Chapter 17

After Mum had gone I went up to my room, stretched out on the bed and did a bit of thinking. I was quite calm. No racing pulse or anything. I didn't feel on top of the world but I didn't feel bad. To tell the truth the meeting had been a bit of an anticlimax. Mum had grown both older and younger – if that's possible. Oddly, though, she seemed to have no real idea of the suffering she'd inflicted, or any real regret – let alone remorse – for running out on us like that. Oh well, we're all made differently. She was obviously happy and leading the kind of life she'd always wanted. She had soothed whatever conscience she had by asking me to go and live with her and Jack but when I refused she hadn't pressed it. Could be that she was even slightly relieved. After all, three years is a long time.

As for me, three summers on I'd changed from a scared kid into a reasonably confident person with a definite goal for the future – which didn't include restoring antiques in Bournemouth! Unfortunately my breakdown had left me with a legacy of phobias which I would probably have for the rest of my life, but events at Finchings had shown me that I was strong enough to cope with them now.

The real problem, as I saw it, was Dad. The divorce would be a terrible blow to his pride. However, I guessed that once the legal break had been made he'd soon settle down again. Mum was right about one thing; he liked his own company best. Even so, I was glad I would be there when the solicitor's letter arrived. Everyone needs a hand to hold sometime.

At supper Jane and Bill acted in such an unnaturally normal way that I knew they were bursting with curiosity. To put them out of their misery – and because I owed them an explanation – I told them everything. I began by apologizing for the lies about Mum, then I told them about her vanishing act and my going loopy and being given a home tutor and all that. I left out the bit about my infatuation with Mark Field because that was very private, but I told them about how I'd lost my nerve and decided not to go back to school, adding that I'd now changed my mind because I wanted to get my final exams. Then I stopped, having run out of breath.

'Your soup's getting cold,' Bill said. 'Eat up.'

I ignored him. 'You did it really,' I said to Jane. 'When you said I could train to teach kids like we have here. I suddenly knew that's what I wanted to do.'

She nodded. 'I expect you knew all along. I just put it into words.'

'Eat, Nell!' Bill commanded. 'I didn't make this stuff just to have you sit and stare at it.'

I picked up my spoon. 'There's just one thing. Could I come back sometimes and help out in the holidays? I shall miss you all terribly but it won't be so bad if I know I can come back.'

Bill groaned. 'Oh Lord, have we got to put up with you and your dramas again? I don't know if I can stand it.'

Jane grinned. 'It's lucky you know him or you might think he was serious. Of course you can, Nell. How about next Christmas for a start? And if you ever need any advice or help you know where to come.' She made a wry face. 'This soup is too coarse, Bill. I do wish we had a food-processor.'

I mentally fingered Jack's crisp note. Could you buy a food-processor for fifty quid?

After supper I slipped on a jacket and went outside. It was dusk but I could still see the lake glimmering between the trees and I imagined all the water-birds safely gathered on the central island for the night, away from the danger of foxes. A few more days and all these lovely moments at Finchings would be happening without me. But what a summer it had been! Although I'd never worked so hard, I'd never had such fun or been so free to come and go as I liked, plan my own plans, make my own mistakes. If only I hadn't made one particular mistake . . .

'Mind if I sit with you?'

The sound of his voice made me jump about four feet into the air. 'N-no,' I said. 'I mean, do.'

He sat down at the far end of the seat. He looked relaxed and quite amazingly attractive in an open-necked navy shirt and jeans. I noticed he kept the bashed side of his face turned away from me.

'Nights are drawing in,' he said in his slow, deep voice.

I nodded vigorously. 'Aren't they just. This time last week you could see the island in the lake from here.'

'We could see it now if you'd like to walk down there.'

'Okay.'

We went down the terrace steps and strolled along the grassy path Bill had cut in the long, waving grass. A cock pheasant, out too late, suddenly rose up beside us, squawking furiously and flapped away into the trees. Afterwards everything was quiet. I was dying to ask a million questions but something told me to wait. There were depths in Jim I didn't yet understand and unless I was patient and learned to listen, both to what he said and what he didn't say, I'd never plumb them.

'By the by,' he said as we were nearing the lake, 'I'm going to register for that business course this week. Dad's agreed to take on extra help for the busy times and I'll work evenings and weekends when I can.'

'That's tremendous!'

'Yeah. It'll be touch-and-go financially but Mum left a bit of money and we'll have to use that to tide us over. Dad's really quite keen now. Full of plans for the future. You'd be amazed.'

'Smashing.'

'Just thought I'd pop over and tell you.'

'Glad you did.'

We walked on in silence until we reached the landing stage where the boat was moored. Side by side we gazed out over the darkening water. Faint waterbird noises were coming from the island and an occasional fish plopped up in the lake near us.

'My mum turned up today,' I said. 'Isn't that amazing?' I realized that I'd been longing to tell him all evening but I hadn't had the courage to go to the cottage in case he snubbed me again.

'Hey, that must have been a real stunner,' he said. 'How did you feel? How *do* you feel?'

I shrugged. 'Okay I guess. It was a bit of a nothing, really. Funny when I've imagined it so often. She's living with an antique dealer in Bournemouth and wants me to go and live with them.'

'Will you?'

'No. I'm going back to school next week.'

'So soon?'

I turned my head and we looked at each other for the first time that evening. I must say he did look a sight when you could see both sides of his face. His bruises had turned a nasty yellow and there was still a blood-congealed cut on his lip.

He stared at me intently for a moment as if trying to fathom my thoughts, or trying to bring himself to express his feelings. Then he gave a despairing shake of the head and turned away.

'I'm sorry, Nell,' he said, his voice all husky and miserable. 'I don't suppose you'll ever forgive me.'

You could have knocked me down with a feather!

'But I didn't think you'd ever forgive *me*,' I said, and once I'd started I found I couldn't stop. 'You see it wasn't my fault, Jim. I knew something horrible would

136

happen if you went into that caravan. Dan suddenly appeared and dragged me off for a ride on that terrible wheel thing. He wouldn't let me go and I was terrified because of this awful phobia I've got about heights and that. When it finished I was sick all over everywhere and you'd disappeared and I had to get Dan to bring me back here and Bill was furious because I was late and, oh I don't know, the whole thing was a nightmare.' And to my absolute horror I collapsed on to the wooden landing stage and burst into tears.

It was as though a dam had burst and all the pent-up emotions of the day just flooded forth. I was vaguely aware of Jim crouching down beside me, then I felt his arms go round me and I relaxed against his chest and cried and cried until his shirt was soaked through and there were no tears but only dry hiccups left, and my nose was running and I hadn't got a hanky, and nor had he, so he plucked a handful of grass which I used to scrub my face clean. After that I just stayed snugly enfolded in his arms, so warm and protected that I longed to linger there all night. Even so I knew I had to ask a very important question.

'Did you and Dan get into a fight?'

He nodded, his mouth buried in my hair.

'Was it because of me?'

He sighed. 'I suppose so. A mate of mine saw what happened at the fair and the next day he reported it to me. Of course I was mad as hell because I thought you'd gone off with him willingly.'

'Never!' I protested vehemently.

He squeezed me tighter in his arms. 'I know. Anyway, I know all about Dan Glease's haunts so I dug him out and told him what I thought of him. He slugged me and I'm afraid I lost my rag and slugged him back. There was quite a shindig and we were both thrown out. Stupid, really. No one got the best of it. No one ever does.'

'Then why were you so nasty to me when I came to the cottage to explain what had happened?'

He groaned. 'I was so ashamed. I should never have left the fair without you. I spotted you on the wheel with Dan and I thought you were having a great time. I should have known better — specially as you'd said how you hated that sort of thing. I was also pretty angry with myself for getting into a fight. I'm a peaceful guy, yet when it comes to the crunch I'm as violent as the next man.'

Drawing away a little I looked up at his face and gently stroked his poor bruised cheek with the tips of my fingers. He pressed my palm against his mouth.

'You're so sweet,' he said huskily, and taking my face in his hands, as if it was a rare and delicate flower, he kissed me deeply and slowly while funny little shocks of pleasure ran up and down my spine and various bits of me tingled in a way they hadn't before. When we stopped kissing we gazed into each other's eyes. His were as dark and mysterious as the lake water and I knew that if we spent the rest of our lives together I'd never fathom their inky depths, never understand what Jim was thinking from one moment to the next. Perhaps that's what made him so exciting.

We walked slowly back to the house, our arms wrapped around each other. I promised to spend all my free time with him before I left. He promised to take me sailing. I promised to write when I reached home. He promised to drive up and visit me sometimes. There was so much to talk about that it took half an hour to make the short journey from the lake to the front door.

Before I went into the house he kissed me again. And again. And went on kissing me until I was dizzy and breathless and laughing, and finally I tore myself away and shut the door firmly in his face. Fortunately no one was around to see my flushed cheeks and (I guessed) sparkling eyes, and I went straight up to bed, where I went to sleep without washing to preserve the imprint of Jim's kisses on my mouth.

Chapter 18

Marion and I said a private goodbye in my room and we both had a little weep.

'You're a super friend,' she said. 'I'll miss you.'

'Oh yeah!' I sniffed. 'You've got Jaz now.'

She gave a watery grin. 'Sure. But it's not the same, you know. I can't talk to Jaz about Jaz can I?'

'I suppose not. Anyway I'll see you at Christmas when I come back. We'll do the town – you and Jaz and me and Jim.'

She frowned doubtfully. 'Do you think they'll get on?'

'We can but try.'

'By the way,' she pulled an envelope out of her pocket. 'This is a note from Mum. I think it's to thank you for helping Nick so much. You know he's agreed to go back to school?'

'No!' I literally jumped for joy. 'That's really terrific.'

'Yeah. He never told us why but we knew it had something to do with your chat with him. Mum's thrilled. She's a different person.'

I grinned happily. 'I really like your mum. How's er . . . how's Dan?

She giggled. 'The bruises have gone now. I wish I'd seen him and Jim slugging it out in the arcade. Anyway Jim came around yesterday and they went out for a beer together. I guess it's all sweetness and light now.'

I sighed with relief. 'Thank heavens for that.'

'Nell!' Jane's voice rang out in the hall. 'Jim's waiting to take you to the station.'

We bounded downstairs only to find that everyone in the place had turned out to see me off – the kids, the staff, Jane and Bill and, of course, Plod, who pranced around barking idiotically and getting in everyone's way.

Jane shoved a small parcel into my hand as I was getting into the car.

'This came in the post today. It looks rather exciting.' She kissed me and slammed the door shut. 'Bye, Nell. See you at Christmas.'

'See you at Christmas!' everyone yelled and all the kids jumped about like a lot of fleas and Marion blubbed openly and even Bill was moved to blow me a kiss. As for me, although I leaned out of the window and looked back the whole length of the drive I couldn't see a thing for the tears misting my eyes.

When we turned into the road I sat back in the seat and blew my nose. 'What a fuss,' I said, laughing in spite of myself. It made me feel warm and happy to know that everyone liked me. Finchings now felt like my second home — in many ways a more loving one than my real home.

'What's in your parcel?' Jim asked, perhaps in order to distract me.

I tore off the wrapping. Inside was a small white box printed with silver bells and ribbons and inside that lay a piece of iced fruit cake and a card which said, 'With best wishes from Mark and Jackie Field'.

I stared down at it. Only a few weeks ago it would have burned my hand like a live coal; now it lay there looking exactly what it was — a piece of dried-up fruit cake.

'Are you hungry?' I asked Jim.

He glanced sideways. 'I don't go much on fruit cake.'

'Neither do I.' I replaced the lid. 'What shall I do with it?'

'Plod likes fruit cake. It's his favourite food.'

'Great. You can give it to him with best wishes from Mark and Jackie Field.'

We both laughed and I stuffed the box into his pocket.

'When are you coming home to meet my Dad?' I asked.

'I could come the weekend after next but won't he think you're a bit young to have a serious boyfriend?'

I craned my neck round to get a last glimpse of the shining sea before we finally turned inland. 'He may but he'll just have to get used to it won't he?'

'I guess so,' Jim said. 'I guess everyone will.'

Ann de Gale
Hands Off! £1.25

Buzz was in two minds about her summer job – on the one hand it was great to work in a gorgeous big old house on the beach in Norfolk, but on the other, working in a restaurant run by a perfectionist Frenchman was hardly the ideal job for someone who was called 'scatterbrained' even by her family. But spilling the soup turns out to be the least of Buzz's problems. The biggest was Jake, or rather her host's lovely daughter Amanda, when she saw how Jake was looking at Buzz . . .

Anita Eires
Star Dreamer 85p

The only thing Candy really knew about her father was that he was one of the world's great trapeze artists. But that was enough – she was determined to follow him. Her mother forbids her even to think about it but, when Candy discovers gymnastics, it seems the perfect training for her dream life. Soon the time in the gym is all she lives for and everything else is neglected – until 'The Great Karde' himself teaches her a bitter, but necessary, lesson about the 'high life' . . .

Working Girl £1.25

Jane Lovejoy's first day in her first job is a milestone in her life. Working for a large advertising agency is glamorous – even if she *was* only in the accounts department! Then, after joining the agency's social club, Jane rediscovers another attraction, Greg – the gorgeous guy she bumped into on the never-to-be-forgotten day of her final interview. Rumour has it that Greg puts work before pleasure, but when Jane sees him with the most attractive girl in the office, she knows his life isn't *all* work and no play . . .

Jane Pitt
Autumn Always Comes 85p

Falling in love in the summer can happen to anyone. But in a strange country where you can't even speak the language very well falling in love can be the most confusing thing in the world. Or at least, that's what Juanita found when she came to England for the very first time. Her pen pal Sandie's family were so very different from her own – exciting, impulsive and confusing. Especially Barry, Sandie's attractive older brother.

Rainbows for Sale £1.25

The day Lucy saw the rainbow her whole life began to change. For a start, she was sixteen at last. She was in love with Tony and their future stretched before her like a bright ribbon. She was happy. Then the rainbow brought Tom Reynolds into her life . . .

All these books are available at your local bookshop or newsagent, or can be ordered direct from the publisher. Indicate the number of copies required and fill in the form below

....

Name ——————————————————————————————
(Block letters please)

Address ——————————————————————————————

——————————————————————————————————————

Send to CS Department, Pan Books Ltd,
PO Box 40, Basingstoke, Hants
Please enclose remittance to the value of the cover price plus:
35p for the first book plus 15p per copy for each additional book
ordered to a maximum charge of £1.25 to cover postage and
packing
Applicable only in the UK

While every effort is made to keep prices low, it is sometimes
necessary to increase prices at short notice. Pan Books reserve the
right to show on covers and charge new retail prices which may
differ from those advertised in the text or elsewhere